This book will teach you all the important first steps in the French language and give you plenty of opportunities to practise what you are learning.

Pages 4 and 5 contain a French pronunciation guide and an introduction to grammar. Try out the sounds introduced in the pronunciation guide before you start the main part of the book.

The section on grammar explains basic grammar words. It will help you if you do not know anything about grammar or if you want to remind yourself of what words like "noun" and "subject" mean.

Page 6 is where the main section starts. Each double page explains certain points about French, so your knowledge will build up as you go through the book.

On each double page, the characters in the picture strips say things that show how the language works in practice. The Speech bubble key gives you translations of what they are saying, but you should try to understand them first, and only use the key for checking. Any new French words that crop up are shown in a list with their English translations, and there is always at least one test-yourself quiz to help you try out what you have learned. (The answers are given on pages 56–57.)

In the Speech bubble key, you will sometimes notice a slightly different translation to the word-for-word one. This is because different languages do not always say things in the same way, and the translation given is more natural in English.

The characters

In this book, you will meet various characters. You can see the main ones on this page.

The first two you will meet are Luc and Céline, as they fly in to Tourville from Paris. They are on their way to the Camembert house where they are going to spend a short holiday. Follow their story as you progress through the book.

Luc Meunier

Céline's brother.
Likes walking, climbing, cycling and eating.

Céline Meunier

Luc's sister.
One year older than him.
Likes reading crime novels.

Marion Camembert

Luc and Céline's friend.
Met them while on holiday last year.

Aline Camembert

Marion's mother.
Quite a well – known sculptress.
Runs the house on a shoe-string budget.

Alain Camembert

Marion's father.
Son of Joseph Camembert.
Works for a charity.

Félix Filou

A well-travelled crook.
On file at Paris headquarters.

Toudou

The Camembert dog.
Tireless and brave, if a bit excitable at times.

Minou

The Camembert cat.
Inquisitive, likes being pampered.
Loves teasing Toudou.

Key

This book uses a few shortened words and symbols that you need to know about:

[m] after a word means it is masculine, **[f]** means it is feminine and **[pl]** means it is plural;
* after a verb means it is irregular.
(Words like "masculine" or "irregular" will be explained when you need them.)

French pronunciation guide

Pronunciation is how words sound. In French, many letters are not said in the same way as in English. French also has groups of letters that are said in a special way.

The list below shows you how letters and groups of letters are usually said. Letters missing from the list sound the same or nearly the same as in English. Bear in mind, though, that there are exceptions and also that people say things differently depending on where they come from.

Learn these tips little by little and try out the words given as examples. If you can get a French speaker to help you, ask them to make the sounds and say the words so that you can copy what you hear.

Vowel sounds

a sounds like "a" in "cat", for example when used in *la*;

e, **eu** and **œu** sound about the same. They sound a bit like the "u" sound in "fur", for example in *je, leur, œuf*. At the end of words that are longer than *je* or *me*, **e** is silent. Before two consonants, **e** usually sounds like **è**, for example in *elle* and *est*;

é sounds a bit like the "a" sound in "late" or the "ai" in "said", for example in *été*;

è, **ê** and **ai** sound like the "ai" sound in "air", for example in *mère, être, aimer*;

i and **y** sound like "ee" in "see", but shorter, for example in *merci, stylo*;

o sounds like "o" in "soft", for example in *port*;

ô, **au** and **eau** sound like "au" in "autumn", for example in *pôle, jaune, bateau*;

ou sounds like "oo" in "mood", for example in *tour*;

oi sounds like "wa" in "wagon", for example in *noir*;

u, as in *tu*, is a sharp "u" sound, but without the "yuh" sound that English puts in front of "u". Round your lips to say "oo", try to say "ee" and you will be close;

ui sounds like the "wee" in "weep", but shorter, for example in *huit*.

Nasal sounds

French has a set of sounds written with a vowel + "n" or "m". The sounds are a bit nasal, or made slightly through the nose as if you had a cold, and you do not voice the "n" or "m".

an and **en** are like the "au(n)" sound in "aunt", for example in *blanc, lent*. **am** and **em** (when before "b" or "p") sound the same, for example in *chambre, emporter*;

ain and **ein** sound a bit like "a(n)" in "can", for example in *maintenant, plein*. **in** sounds the same if it is before a consonant or on the end of a word, for example in *magasin, indice*. **im** also sounds like **ain/ein** if it is before "p" or "b", for example in *impossible*;

on sounds a bit like "o(n)" in "song", for example in *pardon*. **om** is the same, for example in *ombre*;

un (on the end of a word or before a consonant) sounds a bit like "an" when you say "an apple", for example in *lundi*.

Consonants

c is hard as in "cat", for example in *sac*. However, before "i" or "e" and when it is written **ç**, it is soft like "s" in "sun", for example in *merci, ça*. The sign that makes a "c" soft is called a cedilla;

ch sounds like "sh" in "shoes", for example in *chat*;

g is like in "go", for example in *gauche*. However, before "e" or "i" it sounds like the soft "j" sound in "measure", for example in *plage*. **j** is said like this soft **g**, for example *jaune*;

gn is like the "nio" sound in "onion", for example in *gagner*;

h is not sounded at all, for example in *heure*;

ll is usually said as in English, but when it follows "i" it sounds like the "y" in "you", for example in *fille*;[1] a single **l** sometimes sounds the same, particularly when it is after **ai** or **ei** and on the end of a word, for example in *travail* and *soleil*;

qu is the same sound as the hard **c** – like "c" in "cat" – and the "u" is silent, for example in *qui*;

r is a sort of growling "r" sound made in the back of the throat, for example in *mère*;

s sounds like the "z" in "zoo" when it is between two vowels, for example in *trésor*. Otherwise it sounds like "s" in "soap" (the same sound as **ç**), for

1 There are exceptions, for example in *ville, village* and *mille*, "ll" sounds like a normal "ll".

LEARN FRENCH

Nicole Irving

Designed by Russell Punter
Illustrated by Ann Johns

Language consultants : Renée Chaspoul & Danièle Cowen

Series editor : Corinne Stockley
Editorial assistance from Lynn Bresler

Contents

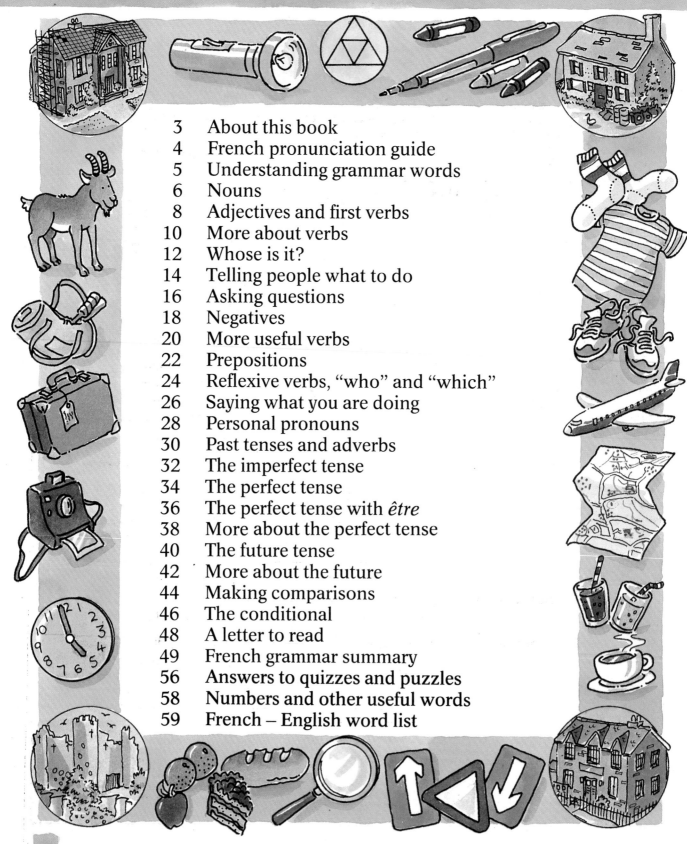

example in *espérer*, *sur*. **ss** always sounds like this, for example in *aussi*.

Words ending in consonants

Most consonants are not usually sounded when they are on the end of a word, so *petit* ends in "tee". However, they are often gently sounded if the next word begins with a vowel – so for *un petit ami* you say "a(n) puteetamee".

Many words end in **er**, **et** or **ez**. This sounds just like **é** and the consonant is usually not sounded, for example in *aller*, *et*, *cherchez*.

With short words like *les*, *des* or *mes*, the **es** ending sounds just like **é**. If words like these come before a vowel, the **s** is sounded like a soft "z", so *les affaires* is said "laizafair". The **x** on the end of *aux* is sounded in just the same way, so *aux autres* sounds like "auzautr".

Accents

As you can see in the list above, French has a few **accents**, or special signs that are added over a vowel. The three French accents are ´ ` ^. They most often go over an "e" and make it sound different from a simple **e**. On other vowels, they do not change the sound, though the hat-shaped accent usually makes the sound longer.

You sometimes see ¨ over **e**, **i** or **u**. It means the vowel is said separately from the one before it (and **ë** is said like **ê**), for example in *Noël*, *aïe*.

Grammar is the set of rules that summarize how a language works. It is easier to learn how French works if you know a few grammar words.

All the words we use when we speak or write can be split up into different types.

A **noun** is a word for a thing, an animal or a person, for example "box", "idea", "invention", "cat", "woman". A noun is **plural** when you are talking about more than one, for example "boxes", "ideas" or "women".

A **pronoun** is a word that stands in for a noun, for example, "he", "you", "me", "yours". If you say "The dog stole your hamburger" and then, "He stole yours", you can see how "he" stands in for "dog" and "yours" stands in for "hamburger".

An **adjective** is a word that describes something, usually a noun, for example "pink", as in "a pink shirt".

A **verb** is an action word, for example "make", "run", "think", "eat". Verbs can change depending on who is doing the action, for example "I make", but "he makes", and they have different **tenses** according to when the action takes place, for example "I make" but "I made". The **infinitive** form of the verb is its basic form, for example "to make", "to run" or "to eat". Dictionaries and word lists normally list verbs in their infinitive form.

An **adverb** is a word that gives extra information about an action.

Many adverbs describe how a verb's action is done, for example "slowly", as in "She opens the box slowly". Other adverbs say when an action happens, for example "yesterday", or where, for example "here".

Prepositions are link words like "to", "at", "for", "towards" and "near".

Subject or object?

When used in a sentence, a noun or pronoun can have different parts to play. It is the **subject** when it is doing the action, for example "the dog" in "The dog barks" or "he" in "He barks". It is the **direct object** when the action is done to it, for example "the dog" in "He brushes the dog" or "him" in "He brushes him".

There is also an **indirect object**. In "He gives the dog a bone", "the dog" is an indirect object ("a bone" is the direct object). You can normally tell an indirect object because it could have a preposition, such as "to", "at" or "from", in front of it, so in the example above, you could say "He gives a bone to the dog". A pronoun can also be an indirect object, for example "him" in "Give him the bone", which can also be said "Give the bone to him".

Nouns

In French, all nouns are either masculine or feminine. This is called their gender. The words for "the" and "a" show the gender.

"The" is *le* with masculine nouns and *la* with feminine nouns, but it is *l'* with all nouns that begin with a vowel and most nouns that begin with an "h". "A" is *un* with masculine nouns and *une* with feminine nouns.

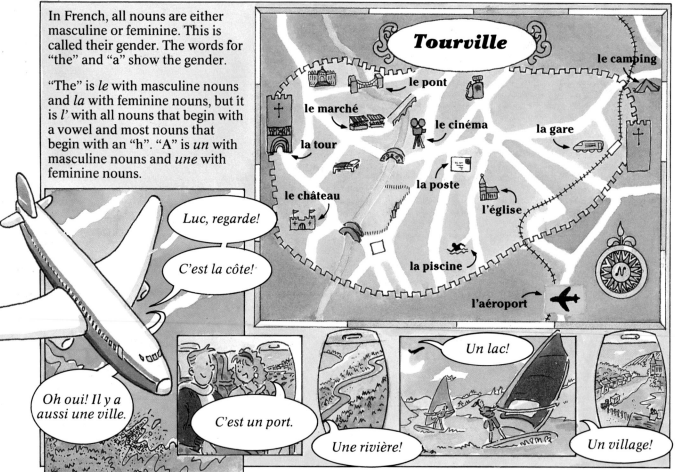

Tourville

le camping

le pont

le marché

le cinéma

la gare

la tour

le château

la poste

l'église

la piscine

l'aéroport

Luc, regarde!

C'est la côte!

Oh oui! Il y a aussi une ville.

C'est un port.

Une rivière!

Un lac!

Un village!

Plural nouns

In the plural, most French nouns add an "s" on the end, "the" is always *les* and "some" is *des*,[1] whatever the gender. Some nouns have unusual plurals, though, such as *le château* (castle) which becomes *les châteaux* (castles).[2]

How to say *les* and *des*

In French, you don't normally pronounce a consonant on the end of a word (see page 5). This means that you don't hear the "s" on *les* and *des* ("lai" and "dai"). However you often do pronounce such a consonant if it comes before a vowel. For example, you say *les îles* and *des îles* with a soft "z" sound in the middle ("laizeel", "daizeel").

Regarde! C'est Tourville.

Oh, des montagnes!

Oui, voilà les ponts...

et les deux tours.

Oh, voilà l'aéroport.

1 Note that English often leaves out "some" where French uses *des*, e.g. *Des montagnes!* (Mountains!). 2 For more about plural nouns, see page 49.

Qu'est-ce que c'est,[3] Céline?

Chouette! Des bonbons.

Et voici la maison Camembert.

C'est la carte.

Learning tip

Try and learn nouns with *le* or *la* in front of them so that you know their gender. With nouns that begin with a vowel, learn them with *un* or *une*. Many words change to match the noun's gender, so getting this right helps to get other words right.

New words

le pont	bridge
le marché	market
la tour	tower
le château(x)	castle
le cinéma	cinema
la poste	post office
le camping	campsite
la gare	station
l'église [f]	church
la piscine	swimming pool
l'aéroport [m]	airport
la côte	coast
la ville	town
le port	port
la rivière	river
le lac	lake
le village	village
l'île [f]	island
la montagne	mountain
le bonbon	sweet, candy
la carte	map
la maison	house
l'hôtel [m]	hotel
le café	café, coffee
la ferme	farm
la route	road
le chemin	path, lane, way
le champ	field
la forêt	forest
regarde	look
c'est	it is, this/that is
ce sont	they are, these/those are
oui	yes
il y a	there is/are
aussi	too, also, as well, (just) as
voilà	there's, there are
voici	here's, here are
et	and
deux	two
chouette	great
qu'est-ce que (c'est)?[3]	what (is it/this/that?)

Getting to the Camembert house

For some strange reason, the man in the seat behind Luc and Céline is looking at their map and memorizing the route to the Camembert house. He's worked out the first of the six landmarks that show the way from the airport. Can you work out the other five? List them in French, making sure you use the right word for "a".

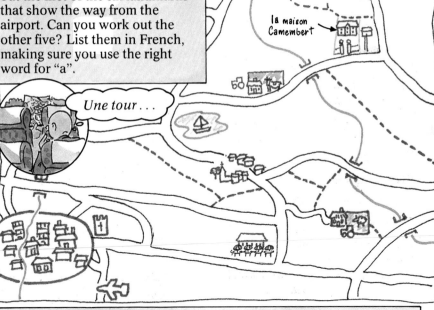

Une tour . . .

la maison Camembert

Speech bubble key

- *Luc, regarde!* Luc, look!
- *C'est la côte!* It's the coast!
- *Oh oui! Il y a aussi une ville.* Oh yes! There's a town too.
- *C'est un port.* It's a port.
- *Une rivière!* A river!
- *Un lac!* A lake!
- *Un village!* A village!
- *Oh, des montagnes!* Oh, mountains!
- *Regarde! C'est Tourville.* Look! That's Tourville.
- *Oui, voilà les ponts . . .* Yes, there are the bridges . . .
- *et les deux tours.* and the two towers.
- *Oh, voilà l'aéroport.* Oh, there's the airport.
- *Chouette! Des bonbons.* Great! Sweets.
- *Qu'est-ce que c'est, Céline?* What's that, Céline?
- *C'est la carte.* It's the map.
- *Et voici la maison Camembert.* And here's the Camembert house.

3 This is pronounced "kess-ke(r)-ssai".

Adjectives and first verbs

Most French adjectives come after the noun (though a few come before).[1] They also agree with the noun. This means that if the noun is feminine or plural, so is the adjective. In the feminine, most adjectives add "e" and in the plural, they add "s" (or "es" in the feminine plural). A few adjectives don't change in the feminine[2] and a few have a more complicated change that you have to learn.

Verbs

French has regular verbs that follow patterns (see page 10) and irregular verbs that don't. *Avoir* (to have) and *être* (to be) are irregular. You will use these verbs a lot. You can find their present tense on this page.

Des vacances parfaites

Un ciel bleu

Une mer bleue

Une plage blanche

TOURVILLE

Des excursions passionnantes

Avoir (to have)

j'ai	I have (got)
tu as	you have (got)
il/elle a	he/she/it has (got)
nous avons	we have (got)
vous avez	you have (got)
ils/elles ont	they have (got)

Tu or *vous*? *Il* or *elle*?

As you can see, French has two words for "you". You say *tu* to a friend. *Vous* is polite and used for an older person or someone you don't know well. *Vous* is also the plural in all cases.

"It" is *il* or *elle* to match the noun's gender. "They" is *ils* in the masculine, *elles* in the feminine and *ils* for a mixture of both.

Être (to be)

je suis	I am
tu es	you are
il/elle est	he/she/it is
nous sommes	we are
vous êtes	you are
ils/elles sont	they are

J'ai un petit sac noir.

Pst, Luc! Tu as aussi une tente.

Ah oui, j'ai une tente verte.

Oh, pardon!

Allô Marion? C'est Céline.

Ah... Je suis fatiguée...

Une valise verte... un sac bleu...

J'ai un sac vert.

Oh, il est grand.

Nous sommes à Tourville...

Merci. Vous êtes bien gentille.

---

8 **1** Adjectives that come before the noun are marked † in the New words list, and there is a list of them on page 50. **2** For example, adjectives that end in "e" never change in the feminine.

My, your, his, her . . .

These words are a special kind of adjective. The word that is used depends on the gender of the noun:

(m)	(f)	(pl)	
mon[3]	ma	mes	my
ton[3]	ta	tes	your
son[3]	sa	ses	his/her/its
notre	notre	nos	our
votre	votre	vos	your
leur	leur	leurs	their

Mon sac à dos est rouge.

C'est ton sac.

Mais non, c'est son sac.

Voici votre valise, Mademoiselle.

Mes valises sont grises.

Non, ça va. Nous avons ta carte.

What is their luggage like?

Try to find these people in the picture strips and work out what their luggage is like (what kind of bag they have and what colour it is). The first solution is *Son sac est vert*.

Speech bubble key

- *J'ai un petit sac noir.* I've got a small black bag.
- *Pst, Luc! Tu as aussi une tente.* Hey, Luc! You've got a tent as well.
- *Ah oui, j'ai une tente verte.* Oh yes, I've got a green tent.
- *Oh, pardon!* Oh, sorry!
- *Oh, il est grand.* Oh, he's tall.
- *Ah . . . Je suis fatiguée . . .* Ah . . . I'm tired . . .
- *Une valise verte . . . un sac bleu . . .* A green suitcase . . . a blue bag . . .
- *J'ai un sac vert.* I've got a green bag.
- *Allô Marion? C'est Céline.* Hello, Marion? It's Céline.

- *Nous sommes à Tourville . . .* We're in Tourville . . .
- *Merci. Vous êtes bien gentille.* Thank you. You are so kind.
- *Non, ça va. Nous avons ta carte.* No, it's all right. We've got your map.
- *Mon sac à dos est rouge.* My backpack is red.
- *C'est ton sac.* This is your bag.
- *Mais non, c'est son sac.* No it's not, it's his bag.
- *Mes valises sont grises.* My suitcases are grey.
- *Voici votre valise, Mademoiselle.* Here's your suitcase, Miss.

New words

les vacances [f]	holidays, vacations
le ciel	sky
la plage	beach
la mer	sea
l'excursion [f]	outing, trip
le sac	bag
la tente	tent
la valise	suitcase
le sac à dos	backpack, rucksack
la serviette	briefcase
parfait(e)	perfect
bleu(e)	blue
blanc(he)	white
passionnant(e)	exciting
petit(e)†	small, little
noir(e)	black
vert(e)	green
pardon	sorry, excuse me
grand(e)†	big, large, tall
fatigué(e)	tired
allô	hello (used on phone)
à	in, at, to
merci	thank you
bien	well, very, most, really, so[4]
gentil(le)	kind, nice
non	no
ça va	(it's) all right
rouge	red
mais	but
gris(e)	grey
Mademoiselle	Miss
jaune	yellow
marron[5]	brown

3 *Mon*, *ton* and *son* are also used in front of feminine nouns that begin with a vowel or "h". 4 *Bien* is often used to reinforce the meaning of adjectives. 5 *Marron* is one of a few adjectives that never change at all.

More about verbs

Most French verbs follow patterns. The standard one is the "er" pattern on the right. You can spot verbs that work like this because their infinitive, or basic form, ends in "er", for example *marcher*. To make the present tense, you add a set of endings to the verb's stem (the infinitive minus "er").

Marcher (to walk)

je marche	I walk/am walking[1]
tu marches	you walk/are walking
il/elle marche	he/she/it walks/is walking
nous marchons	we walk/are walking
vous marchez	you walk/are walking
ils/elles marchent	they walk/are walking

Tu marches trop lentement.

Mais non, je regarde le paysage.

Ah oui, le soleil brille . . .

. . . et les oiseaux chantent.

Pardon, nous cherchons le camping.

C'est facile! Vous continuez tout droit.

Vouloir (to want)

This is a very useful verb. It is irregular (it does not follow a pattern):

je veux	I want
tu veux	you want
il/elle veut	he/she/it wants
nous voulons	we want
vous voulez	you want
ils/elles veulent	they want

Being polite

When you want to ask for something politely, you use *vouloir* in a special tense, and say *je voudrais* (I would like). See page 44.

To say "please", you have to choose between *s'il te plaît*, which you say to a friend, and the polite (or plural) *s'il vous plaît*.

Je veux une table à l'ombre.

Je veux une limonade glacée.

"I want to . . ."

You can use *vouloir* with another verb to say what you want to do, for example *je veux manger* (I want to eat). The second verb is left in the infinitive. You can do the same with *voudrais* and say *Je voudrais manger* (I'd like to eat).

Il veut un thé.

Je voudrais une limonade.

Nous voulons une glace et un jus d'orange.

Et moi, je voudrais un coca, s'il vous plaît.

Je voudrais payer, s'il vous plaît.

Où est mon appareil-photo?

Qu'est-ce que vous voulez faire maintenant?

Je veux visiter le château.

Je veux regarder les magasins.

Oh!

1 English has two present tenses. You can either say "I walk" or "I'm walking". French has only one, so you say *je marche*.

Speech bubble from cartoon (part of image):
Nous voulons louer des bicyclettes.

The mysterious letter

Céline saw the man drop a letter. This is it. It was written by someone who was really tired and it has lots of mistakes (8 in all). Can you rewrite it correctly and work out its meaning in English?

Une île déserte, 1893

Mon cher fils Joseph,

Je suis un vieil homme. Je suis seule sur mon île désert et mon maison près de Tourville est vide. J'ai un secret. Je suis très riches. Maintenant mon trésor est ta trésor. Ma maison cachent le premier indice. D'abord tu cherche les deux bateau.

Adieu,

Clément Camembert

New words

le paysage	landscape
le soleil	sun
l'oiseau(x) [m]	bird
la table	table
la limonade	lemonade
le thé	(cup of) tea
la glace	ice cream
le jus d'orange	orange juice
le coca	Coke
l'appareil-photo [m]	camera
le magasin	shop
la bicyclette	bicycle
le fils	son
l'homme [m]	man
le secret	secret
le trésor	treasure
l'indice [m]	clue
le bateau(x)	ship, boat
regarder	to look (at)
briller	to shine
chanter	to sing
chercher	to look for
continuer	carry on, continue
manger	to eat
payer*	to pay
faire*	to do
visiter	to visit
louer	to hire
cacher	to hide
trop	too
lentement	slowly
facile	easy, simple
tout droit	straight ahead
à l'ombre	in the shade
glacé(e)	ice-cold
moi	me, as for me
s'il te/vous plaît	please
où?	where?
maintenant	now
désert(e)	deserted, desert
cher (chère)	dear
vieux/vieil[2] (vieille)	old
seul(e)	alone
sur	on
près de	near
vide	empty
très	very
riche	rich, wealthy
premier (première)	first
d'abord	first of all
adieu	farewell

* Remember, an asterisk (*) means the verb is irregular.

Speech bubble key

- *Tu marches trop lentement.* You're walking too slowly.
- *Mais non, je regarde le paysage.* No I'm not, I'm looking at the landscape.
- *Ah oui, le soleil brille . . .* Oh yes, the sun's shining . . .
- *. . . et les oiseaux chantent. . . .* and the birds are singing.
- *Pardon, nous cherchons le camping.* Excuse me, we're looking for the campsite.
- *C'est facile! Vous continuez tout droit.* That's easy! You carry on straight ahead.
- *Je veux une table à l'ombre.* I want a table in the shade.
- *Je veux une limonade glacée.* I want an ice-cold lemonade.
- *Il veut un thé.* He wants a cup of tea.
- *Nous voulons une glace et un jus d'orange.* We want an ice cream and an orange juice.
- *Je voudrais une limonade.* I'd like a lemonade.
- *Et moi, je voudrais un coca, s'il vous plaît.* And me, I'd like a Coke please.
- *Je voudrais payer, s'il vous plaît.* I'd like to pay, please.
- *Où est mon appareil-photo?* Where's my camera?
- *Qu'est-ce que vous voulez faire maintenant?* What do you want to do now?
- *Je veux visiter le château.* I want to visit the castle.
- *Je veux regarder les magasins.* I want to look at the shops.
- *Nous voulons louer des bicyclettes.* We want to hire some bicycles.

Whose is it?

In French, to say things such as "Luc's jumper" or "Luc's tent", you use *de* (of), so you say *le pull de Luc*, *la tente de Luc*. (You use *d'* in front of a vowel or an "h".) To say "It's Luc's" or just "Luc's", you use *à* (at, to) and say *Il* (or *elle* or *c'*) *est à Luc* or *À Luc*.

Using *de* and *à* with nouns

You also use *de* with nouns such as "girl" to say things such as "the girl's jumper" – *le pull de la fille* (word for word, "the jumper of the girl"). However, *de* and the French for "the" join up in two cases: *de + le* become *du*, and *de + les* become *des*. This means that, for "of the", you either say *du*, *de la*, *de l'* or *des*.[1]

To say just "It's the girl's" or "The girl's" (for example, in answer to "Whose is it?"), you use *à* – *Il* (or *elle* or *c'*) *est à la fille*, or *À la fille*. Like *de*, *à* joins with *le* and *les* to become *au* and *aux*. This means you either say *au*, *à la*, *à l'* or *aux*.

Appartenir à (to belong to)

This verb is another way to say that something belongs to someone. It follows the pattern of the useful irregular verb *tenir* shown below. Just put "appar" in front of the form you need, for example *il appartient à* (he/it belongs to).

> Bonjour. Nous sommes les amis de Marion.

> Bonjour. Je suis sa mère.

> Je m'appelle Aline... et voici notre chien, Toudou.

> À qui est ce chat?

> Il est à Marion. Il s'appelle Minou.

Tenir (to hold)

je tiens	I hold
tu tiens	you hold
il/elle tient	he/she/it holds
nous tenons	we hold
vous tenez	you hold
ils/elles tiennent	they hold

> Voici la chambre de mes parents,...

> ma chambre et...

> la chambre du locataire.

> Voici ma pièce préférée.

> C'est l'atelier de ma mère.

> C'est le portrait du grand-père de Marion, Joseph.

This, that, these

French doesn't make the difference between "this" and "that" as in "this cat" or "that cat". With masculine nouns, you say *ce* (*ce chat* – this/that cat), or *cet* if the noun begins with a vowel or "h". With feminine nouns you say *cette* and with plural nouns, *ces* (these).

> C'est un vieux tableau de la maison Camembert.

> Oh non, c'est Mangetout, la chèvre des voisins!

> À qui appartiennent ces vêtements?

> Ils sont à mon frère...

1 *Du*, *de la*, *de l'* and *des* can also mean "some" or "any". For more about this, see page 20.

et ce pull . . .

J'aime bien ces lunettes.

À qui est cette chemise?

Il appartient au maçon.

Elles sont à Céline.

À Luc.

Et ces jumelles?

Elles sont aussi à Luc.

Les vêtements

les vêtements [m]	clothes
le pantalon	trousers
le jean	jeans
la jupe	skirt
la robe	dress
le survêtement	track suit
le short	shorts
le pull	jumper
le sweat-shirt	sweatshirt
la chemise	shirt
le tee-shirt	T-shirt
la veste	jacket
le costume	suit
la chaussette	sock
le collant	tights
la chaussure	shoe
les baskets [f]	trainers
les bottes [f]	boots
le chapeau(x)	hat

Saying what you like

The best way to say "I like" is *j'aime* from the verb *aimer* (to like, to love). This follows the standard "er" pattern (see page 10). You often add *bien* (well) after it when all you mean is "to like". This is because, on its own, it can often mean "to love", especially when you are talking about people. Notice how *je* (I) shortens to *j'* before a vowel (it also often does so before an "h").

New words

l'ami [m]²	friend
la mère	mother
le père	father
la grand-mère	grandmother
le grand-père	grandfather
l'arrière-grand-père [m]	great-grandfather
le chien	dog
le chat	cat
la fille	girl, daughter
le garçon	boy
la chambre	(bed)room
les parents [m]	parents
le locataire	lodger
la pièce	room
l'atelier [m]	studio
le tableau(x)	painting
le portrait	portrait
la chèvre	goat
le voisin	neighbour
le frère	brother
la sœur	sister
le maçon	builder
les lunettes [f]	glasses
les jumelles [f]	binoculars
l'outil [m]	tool
je m'appelle³	my name is (I am called)
il s'appelle³	his/its name is (he/it is called)
aimer	to like, to love
bonjour	hello
à qui?	whose? to who(m)?
préféré(e)	favourite

Speech bubble key

- *Bonjour. Nous sommes les amis de Marion.* Hello. We're Marion's friends.
- *Bonjour. Je suis sa mère.* Hello. I'm her mother.
- *Je m'appelle Aline . . . et voici notre chien, Toudou.* My name's Aline . . . and this is our dog, Toudou.
- *À qui est ce chat?* Whose cat is that?
- *Il est à Marion. Il s'appelle Minou.* He's Marion's. His name's Minou.
- *Voici la chambre de mes parents, . . . ma chambre et . . . la chambre du locataire.* Here's my parents' bedroom, . . . my room and . . . the lodger's room.
- *Voici ma pièce préférée.* Here's my favourite room.
- *C'est l'atelier de ma mère.* It's my mother's studio.
- *C'est un vieux tableau de la maison Camembert.* That's an old painting of Camembert house.

- *C'est le portrait du grand-père de Marion, Joseph.* That's a portrait of Marion's grandfather, Joseph.
- *Oh non, c'est Mangetout, la chèvre des voisins!* Oh no, it's Mangetout, the neighbours' goat!
- *À qui appartiennent ces vêtements?* Who do these clothes belong to?
- *Ils sont à mon frère . . .* They're my brother's . . .
- *et ce pull . . .* and this jumper . . .
- *Il appartient au maçon.* It belongs to the builder.
- *J'aime bien ces lunettes.* I like these glasses.
- *Elles sont à Céline.* They're Céline's.
- *À qui est cette chemise?* Whose shirt is this?
- *À Luc.* It's Luc's.
- *Et ces jumelles?* And these binoculars?
- *Elles sont aussi à Luc.* They're Luc's as well.

À qui est . . . ?

Try to find these things in the picture strips and work out whose they are. (The answer to the first one is *Ce survêtement est à Marion.*)

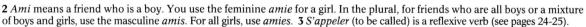

2 *Ami* means a friend who is a boy. You use the feminine *amie* for a girl. In the plural, for friends who are all boys or a mixture of boys and girls, use the masculine *amis*. For all girls, use *amies*. 3 *S'appeler* (to be called) is a reflexive verb (see pages 24-25).

Telling people what to do

To tell someone what to do (for example, "Wait!"), you use the imperative of the verb. To make this in French, you normally use the verb's present tense in either the *tu* or *vous* form (see page 8), but you leave out the words *tu* and *vous*. With "er" verbs you also drop the "s" from the end of the *tu* form, for example, *tu marches* becomes *Marche!* (Walk!).[1]

Useful imperatives

Here is a list of imperatives that are used very often. Some of them come from irregular verbs, and some from reflexive verbs:[2]

tu form	*vous* form	
va	allez	go (from *aller*)
sois	soyez	be (from *être*)
fais	faites	do (from *faire*)
dépêche-toi	dépêchez-vous	hurry up (from *se dépêcher*[2])
prends	prenez	take (from *prendre*)
viens	venez	come (from *venir*)
tais-toi	taisez-vous	be quiet (from *se taire*[2])
suis	suivez	follow (from *suivre*)

Attention! Va doucement.

Lance la corde.

Sois sage, Toudou.

Fais attention!

Allez! Tirez!

Fermez vite la barrière, Madame.[3]

Reste tranquille, Mangetout.

Dépêchez-vous!

Saying what you must do

Devoir (to have to, must) is a useful irregular verb for saying what you must do. It is used with the infinitive of another verb, for example *Je dois fermer la barrière* (I must shut the gate).

Devoir (to have to, must)

je dois	I must
tu dois	you must
il/elle doit	he/she/it must
nous devons	we must
vous devez	you must
ils/elles doivent	they must

Il faut

Il faut is often used with the infinitive of another verb to mean "you must" in the general sense of "it is necessary to", "people have to", "one must". You also use it instead of *nous devons* for "we must".

Il faut tout visiter – la vieille église, les grottes, Port-le-Vieux . . .

Moi, je dois vite faire des courses à Port-le-Vieux.

À tout à l'heure.

Il faut fermer la barrière.

Tourne à gauche . . .

et prends le premier chemin à droite.

Toudou, viens ici!

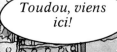

1 Dropping the "s" does not alter the sound of the word. 2 You can find out about reflexive verbs on page 24. 3 To be polite in French, you often use the words *Madame* (Mrs), *Monsieur* (Mr) or *Mademoiselle* (Miss) on their own like this.

Ce doit être la maison Camembert.

Je dois vite trouver cet indice.

D'abord, je dois chercher ma lime.

Tais-toi!

Ces serrures doivent être très vieilles.

Tais-toi, sale chien!

New words

la corde	rope	trouver	to find
la barrière	gate		
la grotte	cave	attention	watch out, careful
la lime	nail file		
la serrure	lock	doucement	slowly
		tranquille	quiet, calm
se dépêcher[2]	to hurry (up)	sage	well behaved, good
se taire*[2]	to be quiet		
rester	to stay, to remain	vite	quickly, fast
lancer	to throw	Madame[3]	Mrs
faire* attention	to watch out, to be careful	tout	everything
		à tout à l'heure	see you later
tirer	to pull	ici	here
fermer	to close, to shut	ce, c'[4]	this, that, it, they
faire* des courses	to do some shopping	sale	dirty, horrible

Directions

The imperative is very useful for giving and understanding directions. Below is a list of useful direction words:

la rue	street	tourner	to turn
la (grande) route	(main) road	traverser	to cross
le chemin	path, lane, way	continuer	to carry on
la place	square		
le carrefour	junction	premier (première)	first
les feux [m]	traffic lights		
le passage clouté	pedestrian crossing	deuxième	second
		troisième	third
aller*	to go	quatrième	fourth
prendre*	to take	tout droit	straight ahead
venir*	to come	à gauche	(to/on the) left
suivre*	to follow	à droite	(to/on the) right

Speech bubble key

- *Attention! Va doucement.* Careful! Go slowly.
- *Reste tranquille, Mangetout.* Keep calm, Mangetout.
- *Lance la corde.* Throw the rope.
- *Sois sage, Toudou.* Behave yourself (/Be good), Toudou.
- *Fais attention!* Watch out!
- *Allez! Tirez!* Go on! Pull!
- *Fermez vite la barrière, Madame.* Shut the gate quickly!
- *Dépêchez-vous!* Hurry!
- *Il faut tout visiter – la vieille église, les grottes, Port-le-Vieux . . .* You must visit everything – the old church, the caves, Port-le-Vieux . . .
- *Moi, je dois vite faire des courses à Port-le-Vieux.* I must quickly do some shopping in Port-le-Vieux.
- *À tout à l'heure.* See you later.
- *Il faut fermer la barrière.* You have to shut the gate.
- *Tourne à gauche . . .* Turn left . . .
- *et prends le premier chemin à droite.* and take the first path on the right.
- *Toudou, viens ici!* Toudou, come here!
- *Ce doit être la maison Camembert.* This must be the Camembert house.
- *Je dois vite trouver cet indice.* I have to find that clue fast.
- *D'abord, je dois chercher ma lime.* First, I must look for my nail file.
- *Tais-toi!* Be quiet!
- *Ces serrures doivent être très vieilles.* These locks must be very old. *Tais-toi, sale chien!* Be quiet, you horrible dog!

The way to the old church

Having taken the first path on the right, Marion, Luc and Céline are here. They need five directions to get to the church. Pretend you're Marion and give Luc and Céline these directions. The first is *Traversez la grande route.*

(Look at the map on page 7.)

4 *Ce* (or *c'*) is only used to mean "this, that, it, they" in a few expressions like *c'est* and *ce doit être*.

Asking questions

There are two main ways of asking questions in French. The easiest is to put *est-ce que*[1] at the start of a sentence, for example *Est-ce que tu as un frère?* (Do you have/Have you got a brother?). The second method is to put the subject ("you" in "you have") after the verb, with a hyphen in between, for example *As-tu un frère?* This method can be used if the subject is *tu, il(s), elle(s), nous* or *vous*, but avoid it with *je*, names and nouns.

Pouvoir (to be able to, can, may)

You often use this irregular verb with another verb in the infinitive to ask if you can or may do something, for example *Est-ce que je peux regarder?* (Can/May I look?).

Pouvoir

je peux	I can
tu peux	you can
il/elle peut	he/she/it can
nous pouvons	we can
vous pouvez	you can
ils/elles peuvent	they can

Est-ce que vous avez des pommes?

Je voudrais deux kilos d'oranges.

Est-ce que tu aimes les fraises?

Est-ce que je peux goûter?

Bonjour, Madame Camembert.

Bonjour, Monsieur.

Avez-vous un panier?

Ce sont des mandarines.

Pardon, pouvez-vous porter ce carton?

Question words

combien (de + noun)?	how much?, how many?
comment?	how?
où?	where?
pourquoi?	why?
quand?	when?
que?[2]	what?[3]
quel(le)?	which?, what?[3]
qui?	who?

How to use question words

With question words, if the subject is *tu, il(s), elle(s), nous* or *vous*, you do the same as when you have no question word, that is, you use either method given above, for example *Où est-ce que tu es?* or *Où es-tu?* (Where are you?). If the subject is *je*, it is best to use the first method. If the subject is a name or noun, use method one for long questions (anything longer than question word + verb + subject) and method two for short questions.

Asking questions the lazy way

In spoken French, you often form questions by just adding ? to a sentence, or a question word and ?, for example *Pourquoi tu es fatigué?* (Why are you tired?). This method is all right for everyday, spoken French.

Quel(le)? (which?)

This changes to match the noun that follows. You use *quel* with a masculine noun, *quelle* with a feminine one, and *quels* or *quelles* in the plural.

Pharmacie Cachet

Pourquoi est-ce que la pharmacie est fermée?

Qu'est-ce que c'est?

Parce que Madame Cachet est malade.

Pardon, où est la boulangerie?

C'est un crabe.

16

1 It sounds like "aiss-ke(r)" The *que* shortens to *qu'* in front of vowels. 2 *Que* drops the "e" before vowels, so used with *est-ce que*, you say *qu'est-ce que*. 3 English confuses "what?" and "which?". *Que?* is "what?" as in "What do you do?". *Quel?* is "which/what?" as in "Which/What flavour?".

Shopping quiz

Try saying all this in French
(using the polite *vous* for "you"):

Where is the supermarket?

I'd like an ice cream. How much do
they cost?
Which flavours have you got?
Can I have a kilo of apples, please?
Can you carry my basket?

New words

la pomme	apple	*le parfum*	flavour
le panier	basket	*la lettre*	letter
le kilo (followed	kilo (of)	*la blague*	joke
by *de/d'* + noun		*la chasse au trésor*	treasure hunt
without "a" or		*le supermarché*	supermarket
"the")		*goûter*	to taste, to have a
l'orange [f]	orange		taste
la mandarine	mandarin	*porter*	to carry, to wear
la fraise	strawberry	*coûter*	to cost
le carton	(cardboard) box	*expliquer*	to explain
la pharmacie	chemist's, pharmacy	*Monsieur*	Mr
la boulangerie	baker's	*fermé(e)*	closed
le magicien	magician	*parce que*	because
le crabe	crab	*malade*	ill, unwell
le gâteau(x)	cake	*vrai(e)*	real, true
le croissant	croissant		

What does the letter mean?

Resting outside the church, Céline remembers the letter the man
dropped at the café . . .

Marion knows who the writer
was, and thinks she knows what
and where the first clue is.
Thinking about it, Luc and Céline
can work it out too. Can you?
Answer these questions and see:

Qui est Clément Camembert?
Que sont "les deux bateaux"? (Look
at the pictures on page 12.)
*Quelle pièce doivent visiter Marion,
Luc et Céline?*

Speech bubble key

- *Bonjour, Madame Camembert.* Hello, Mrs Camembert.
- *Bonjour, Monsieur.* Hello.
- *Est-ce que vous avez des pommes?* Have you got any[4] apples?
- *Avez-vous un panier?* Have you got a basket?
- *Je voudrais deux kilos d'oranges.* I'd like two kilos of oranges.
- *Ce sont des mandarines.* They're mandarins.
- *Est-que tu aimes les fraises?* Do you like strawberries?
- *Est-ce que je peux goûter?* May I have a taste?
- *Pardon, pouvez-vous porter ce carton?* Excuse me, can you carry this box?
- *Pourquoi est-ce que la pharmacie est fermée?* Why is the chemist's closed?
- *Parce que Madame Cachet est malade.* Because Mrs Cachet is ill.
- *Pardon, où est la boulangerie?* Excuse me, where is the baker's?
- *Qu'est-ce que c'est?* What's that?
- *C'est un crabe.* It's a crab.
- *Combien coûtent ces gâteaux?* How much do these cakes cost?
- *Combien de croissants voulez-vous?* How many croissants do you want?
- *Qu'est-ce que tu veux?* What do you want?
- *Est-ce que je peux avoir une glace?* Can I have an ice cream?
- *Quel parfum veux-tu?* What flavour do you want?
- *Qu'est-ce que tu cherches, Céline?* What are you looking for, Céline?
- *Où est-elle? Ah!* Where is it? Ah!
- *Marion, est-ce que tu peux expliquer cette lettre?* Marion, can you explain this letter?
- *Est-ce que c'est une blague?* Is it a joke?
- *Chouette! C'est une vraie chasse au trésor!* Great! It's a real treasure hunt!

4 English changes from "some" to "any" in questions like this. French keeps the word for "some" – here, *des*. For more about "some/any", see page 20.

Negatives

In English, you make verbs negative by using "not", for example "I am not tired". You often also need an extra verb like "do" or "can", for example "I do not know" (or "I don't know"), rather than "I know not".

Ne . . . pas (not)

The French for "not" is *ne . . . pas* (*n'. . . pas* if *ne* is before a vowel or "h"). The words go on either side of the verb, for example *je suis fatigué* becomes *je ne suis pas fatigué* (I am not tired), or *je pense* becomes *je ne pense pas* (I don't think). Notice how you don't need an extra verb like the English "do".

Ne . . . rien, ne . . . personne.

Rien means "nothing" and *personne* means "nobody". With a verb, they mean "not . . . anything" or "nothing" and "not . . . anybody" or "nobody", but you add *ne* (or *n'*) before the verb, for example *Je ne veux rien* (I don't want anything), *Je ne trouve personne* (I can't find anybody). This is also true if *rien* and *personne* are the subject, for example *Rien ne change* (Nothing changes), *Personne ne chante* (Nobody's singing).

Ne . . . pas de (not a, not any, no)

The French for "not a", "not any" or "no" (as in "no bread") is *ne . . . pas de*, or *d'* if the noun begins with a vowel (and sometimes if it begins with an "h"), for instance *Je n'ai pas de chien* (I do not have a dog, I haven't got a dog).

Savoir (to know)

This is another useful irregular verb. You often use it with a verb in the infinitive to mean "I know how to", "I can" (as opposed to "I'm allowed to", "I can"), for example *Je sais nager* (I can swim).

je sais	I know
tu sais	you know
il/elle sait	he/she/it knows
nous savons	we know
vous savez	you know
ils/elles savent	they know

On (we)

You often use *on* instead of *nous* to mean "we", especially in spoken French. It sounds more casual than *nous*. *On* is used with the *il/elle* form of the verb, for instance *on sait*, which means the same as *nous savons*.[2]

> *La porte n'est pas fermée à clé . . .*

> *Mais les bicyclettes ne sont pas là.*

> *Tais-toi, Toudou! Il ne faut pas aboyer si fort!*

> *Qu'est-ce que tu cherches?*

> *Il n'y a[1] personne . . .*

> *Il y a un voleur dans la maison!*

> *Quels bateaux? . . . Je ne trouve pas de bateaux.*

> *Bonsoir, chéri. Bonsoir, Jean.*

> *Bonsoir, chérie . . . Ah zut! Il n'y a pas d'aspirines.*

> *Oui, je sais. C'est parce que la pharmacie est fermée.*

> *Salut, tout le monde!*

> *Je n'ai rien, pas d'aspirines, pas de sparadraps . . .*

> *Oh! Ne regardez pas par ici!*

> *Voici les deux bateaux.*

> *Marion, qui est cet homme?*

> *Je ne sais pas.*

> *Oh, il y a un homme dehors.*

---

1 With *il y a* (there is/are), *n'* always goes before *y*. **2** *On* can also mean "you" in the general sense of "one", e.g. *On ne peut pas entrer par là* (One/you can't go in that way).

> *Ce n'est pas Jean, le locataire...*

> *Où êtes-vous? On dîne!*

> *Regardez! Ils ne sont pas exactement pareils.*

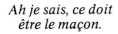

> *Ah je sais, ce doit être le maçon.*

> *Mais le maçon ne porte pas de costume.*

> *OK. On arrive.*

New words

la porte	door
le voleur	burglar
l'aspirine [f], *le cachet (d'aspirine)*	aspirin
le sparadrap	plaster
la carte (à jouer)	(playing) card
le dé	die (pl: dice)
la bougie	candle
le livre	book
le chapeau(x) haut de forme, le haut-de-forme	top hat
penser	to think
changer	to change
*aboyer**	to bark
nager	to swim
dîner	to have supper
arriver	to arrive, to come, to get to

fermé(e) à clé	locked
là	there
si	so
fort	loud(ly)
dans	in
bonsoir	good evening, hello, good-night
chéri [m], *chérie* [f]	darling, dear
zut	blast, damn
salut	hi, hello, bye
tout le monde	everyone, everybody
par ici	this way, over/around here
dehors	outside
exactement	exactly
pareil(le)	(the) same
jamais (ne... jamais)[3]	never (not ever)

The first clue

> *Il n'y a pas de cartes.*

Marion's family have always been puzzled by the two pictures. They did not know Clément Camembert had them painted when he hid his treasure. The six items missing from the second one are the clue to where to go next in the hunt. Marion has spotted the first item. Can you spot the other five (and make five sentences in the same way)?

Marion knows where to go now. Do you?

Speech bubble key

- *La porte n'est pas fermée à clé...* The door isn't locked.
- *Mais les bicyclettes ne sont pas là.* But the bicycles aren't there.
- *Tais-toi, Toudou! Il ne faut pas aboyer si fort!* Be quiet, Toudou! You mustn't bark so loud!
- *Qu'est-ce que tu cherches?* What are you looking for?
- *Il n'y a personne...* There isn't anybody here...
- *Il y a un voleur dans la maison!* There's a burglar in the house!
- *Quels bateaux?... Je ne trouve pas de bateaux.* What ships? I can't find any ships.
- *Bonsoir, chéri. Bonsoir, Jean.* Good evening, darling. Good evening, Jean.
- *Bonsoir, chérie... Ah zut! Il n'y a pas d'aspirines.* Good evening, darling... Oh blast! There aren't any aspirins.
- *Oui, je sais. C'est parce que la pharmacie est fermée.* Yes, I know. That's because the chemist's is closed.
- *Je n'ai rien, pas d'aspirines, pas de sparadraps...* I haven't got anything, no aspirins, no plasters...
- *Salut, tout le monde!* Hi everyone!
- *Oh! Ne regardez pas par ici!* Oh! Don't look over here!
- *Voici les deux bateaux.* Here are the two ships.
- *Oh, il y a un homme dehors.* Oh, there's a man outside.
- *Marion, qui est cet homme?* Marion, who's that man?
- *Je ne sais pas.* I don't know.
- *Ce n'est pas Jean, le locataire...* It's not Jean, the lodger...
- *Ah je sais, ce doit être le maçon.* Oh I know, it must be the builder.
- *Mais le maçon ne porte pas de costume...* But the builder doesn't wear a suit...
- *Où êtes-vous? On dîne!* Where are you? We're eating!
- *OK. On arrive.* OK. We're coming.
- *Regardez! Ils ne sont pas exactement pareils.* Look! They're not exactly the same.

---

3 *Ne... jamais* works like *ne... rien* and *ne... personne*.

More useful verbs

As well as verbs of the "er" pattern (see page 10) and irregular verbs, French has verbs with other patterns. Most of these only affect a few verbs, so it is best to learn the verbs one by one like irregular verbs. However, there are two useful "ir" patterns.

"ir" verbs

Most verbs ending in "ir" (not "oir") follow *choisir*. This means they add the same endings to their stem (infinitive minus "ir"). Here is the present tense of *choisir*.

Choisir (to choose)

je choisis	I choose (am choosing)
tu choisis	you choose
il/elle choisit	he/she/it chooses
nous choisissons	we choose
vous choisissez	you choose
ils/elles choisissent	they choose

Partir (to go (away), to leave)

A few useful "ir" verbs work like *partir*, not *choisir*. They are *dormir*, *mentir*, *sentir*, *servir* and *sortir*.

je pars	I leave (am leaving)
tu pars	you leave
il/elle part	he/she/it leaves
nous partons	we leave
vous partez	you leave
ils/elles partent	they leave

The next day at The Magician Inn . . .

À quelle heure est-ce que tu sors ce soir?

Regarde! Ils finissent ta glace.

Chut! Je réfléchis.

Ça sent bon . . .

Ton train part bientôt.

New words

le soir	evening
le train	train
les frites [f]	chips, French fries
le fromage	cheese
le gosse	kid
la photo	photo
le légume	vegetable
la soupe	soup
dormir	to sleep, to be asleep
mentir	to lie (tell lies)
sentir	to feel, to smell
servir	to serve
sortir	to go out
finir	to finish
réfléchir	to think
comprendre*	to understand
apprendre*	to learn
adorer	to adore, to love
exagérer	to exaggerate, to go too far, to push your luck
gêner	to bother, to be/get in the way
manger	to eat
apporter	to bring
à quelle heure?	what time?
bon(ne)	good, right, nice
bientôt	soon
et puis	and then, and also, and anyhow
ça suffit	that's enough
tout de suite	straight/right away, this instant
prochain(e)	next

More about "some" and "any"

You already know that, with plural nouns, "some" (or "any" in questions) is *des*. With singular nouns, "some/any" is *du* before masculine nouns, *de la* before feminine nouns and *de l'* before nouns that begin with a vowel (and before many that begin with "h"). In English you sometimes leave out "some/any", but you always use it in French, for example *Il veut de la glace* (He wants (some) ice cream). Also remember that in negative sentences, "any" is always *ne . . . pas de* or *d'* (see page 18).

Prendre (to take)

This is an irregular verb. It is often used to mean "to have" when talking about food, for example *Je prends des frites* (I'm having chips). *Comprendre* and *apprendre* have the same endings.

je prends	I take (am taking)
tu prends	you take
il/elle prend	he/she/it takes
nous prenons	we take
vous prenez	you take
ils/elles prennent	they take

Speech bubble key

- *À quelle heure est-ce que tu sors ce soir?* What time are you going out this evening?
- *Regarde! Ils finissent ta glace.* Look! They're finishing your ice cream.
- *Ça sent bon . . .* That smells good . . .
- *Chut! Je réfléchis.* Shhh! I'm thinking.
- *Ton train part bientôt.* Your train's leaving soon.
- *Elle prend du fromage.* She's having cheese.
- *Est-ce que tu prends aussi des frites?* Are you having chips too?
- *Oh oui, j'adore les frites.* Oh yes, I love chips.
- *Je ne mange pas de légumes.* I don't eat vegetables.
- *Ces gosses exagèrent! Ils gênent!* Those kids are pushing their luck! They're getting in the way!
- *Et puis, pourquoi est-ce qu'ils prennent des photos?* And anyhow, why are they taking photos?
- *Attention, il apporte de la soupe.* Watch out, he's bringing some soup.
- *Bon, ça suffit! Sortez tout de suite!* Right, that's enough! Get out this instant!
- *Hep, on part!* Hey, we're going!
- *Hé, regardez! J'ai le prochain indice.* Hey, look! I've got the next clue.

Crossword puzzle

Each solution is one or more French words. The words you need are shown in English in the brackets. Put them in the correct form for the French sentence and they should slot into the puzzle.

Across

1. (He's having) *du fromage.* (2, 5)
5. *Voilà les* (keys) *de la porte.* (4)
6. *Je voudrais* (tea). (2, 3)
7. *La soupe* (smells) *bon.* (4)
8. *Quand est-ce que le train* (leaves)? (4)
10. *Où est* (your) *valise?* (2)
11. *Tais-toi!* (You're lying)! (2, 4)

Down

2. *Nous* (are leaving) *bientôt.* (7)
3. *Je mange* (ice cream). (2, 2, 5)
4. *Je prends* (chips). (3, 6)
7. *Anne* (is going out) *ce soir.* (4)
9. *Je veux* (some) *jus d'orange.* (2)

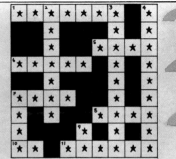

To do the crossword, trace the outline onto a piece of paper but leave out the stars. They show the squares that you have to fill.

Prepositions are words like "in", "on" or "of". Most French ones are easy to use, for example *Ton pull est sous la table* (Your jumper is under the table). Here are the most common ones:

à	at, to
à côté de	next to
après	after
à travers	through
avant	before
avec	with
chez	at the house of, at X's
contre	against
dans	in, into
de	of, from
derrière	behind
devant	in front of
en	in (a language, colour, season or month), (made) of[1]
en face de	opposite
entre	between
hors de	out of
jusqu'à	as far as, up/down to, until
loin de	far from
par	by, through (a window)
pour	for
(tout) près de	(right) near
sous	under
sur	on, onto
vers	towards

De and *à*

Remember that with *le* and *les*, *de* becomes *du* and *des*, and *à* becomes *au* and *aux*. *De* and *à* are used to say whose something is (see page 12), but also in many other ways, for example *Je viens de France* (I come from France), *Je vais à Nice* (I'm going to Nice). With prepositions that end in *de* or *à*, for example *à côté de*, *de* and *à* behave in the usual way, so you say *à côté du café* (next to the café).

Choosing the right preposition

Beware: French does not always use the same preposition as English. For example, to say "on" a bus, train or plane, French uses "in" (*dans*).

Aller and *venir*

These are two useful irregular verbs. *Revenir* (to come back, to return) and *devenir* (to become) are formed like *venir*.

Aller (to go)

je vais	I go (am going)
tu vas	you go
il/elle va	he/she/it goes
nous allons	we go
vous allez	you go
ils/elles vont	they go

Venir (to come)

je viens	I come (am coming)
tu viens	you come
il/elle vient	he/she/it comes
nous venons	we come
vous venez	you come
ils/elles viennent	they come

[1] *En* also means "to" or "in" when used before feminine country names, e.g. *en France* (to/in France). For "to" or "in" before masculine or plural country names, you use *à* + "the". This means you use *au* (*à* + *le*) or *aux* (*à* + *les*), e.g. *au Japon* (to/in Japan), *aux États-Unis* (to/in the United States).

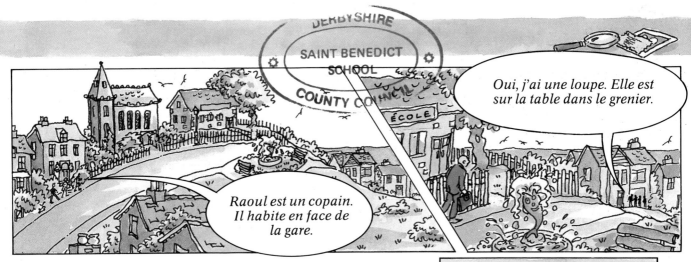

New words

la France	France	le bâtiment	building
la fenêtre	window	la réponse	answer
la sortie	exit	la question	question
la femme	woman	la vache	cow
le jardin	garden	la colline	hill
la fontaine	fountain	l'arbre [m]	tree
le quai	quay		
le filet	net	revenir	to come back, to return
le mot	word, note		
le banc	bench	devenir	to become
la loupe	magnifying glass	poser	to put down
l'idée [f]	idea	habiter	to live
le copain	mate, good friend[2]	le/la/les même(s)	the (very) same
l'école [f]	school	chauve	bald
le grenier	attic	à la maison	(at) home

The clue from the inn

Le prochain indice est dans un bâtiment à Port-le-Vieux. Cherche les réponses à ces questions:

Où est la vache?
Où est le chien?
Où est le banc?
Où est la ferme?

When Marion's friend finally finds his magnifying glass, Luc, Céline and Marion read the note that Luc found in the inn. They have to answer four questions. Luckily the photo Marion took of the painted seat holds the answers. Can you work out the four answers (in French)?

Now can you work out which building they have to go to and finish Céline's sentence? (The four answers apply to only one building in Port-le-Vieux.)

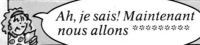
Ah, je sais! Maintenant nous allons *********

Speech bubble key

- *Regardez par la fenêtre!* Look through the window!
- *Près de la sortie . . . à côté de la femme en rouge.* Near the exit . . . next to the woman in red.
- *C'est l'homme de l'aéroport!* It's the man from the airport!
- *C'est l'homme avec la lettre!* It's the man with the letter!
- *C'est l'homme du jardin!* It's the man from the garden!
- *C'est le même homme!* It's the same man!
- *Vite! Il doit vouloir notre trésor.* Quickly! He must want our treasure.
- *Oh non! L'homme chauve! Là, devant la fontaine.* Oh no! The bald man! There, in front of the fountain.
- *Il vient sur le quai.* He's coming onto the quay.
- *Vite, venez derrière ce filet!* Quick, come behind this net!
- *Ça va!* It's OK!
- *Bon, pose le mot et les photos sur ce banc.* Right, put the note and the photos on this bench.
- *Est-ce que tu as une loupe?* Have you got a magnifying glass?
- *Oui, mais à la maison.* Yes, but at home.
- *Ah, j'ai une idée! Venez, on va chez Raoul.* Ah, I know! Come on, we're going to Raoul's.
- *Raoul est un copain. Il habite en face de la gare.* Raoul's a mate. He lives opposite the station.
- *Oui, j'ai une loupe. Elle est sur la table dans le grenier.* Yes, I've got a magnifying glass. It's on the table in the attic.

2 The feminine word is *la copine*.

Reflexive verbs, "who" and "which"

Reflexive verbs are verbs that always begin with words like *me* (myself) or *te* (yourself), and whose infinitive begins with the word *se* or *s'* – see *se lever* below. They can be regular or irregular. Some of them seem logical as they are an action you do to yourself (*se raser* – to shave), but many are reflexive for no obvious reason (*se terminer* – to end, to finish). In either case, English has no real equivalent.[1]

> *Pourquoi est-ce que vous vous cachez?*

> *Parce qu'on n'aime pas l'école.*

Se lever (to get up)

je me lève	I get up (am getting up)
tu te lèves	you get up
il/elle se lève	he/she/it gets up
nous nous levons	we get up
vous vous levez	you get up
ils/elles se lèvent	they get up

The imperative is made in the usual way (see page 14), but you put a hyphen plus *toi* or *vous* after the verb, so you say *Lève-toi* or *Levez-vous* (Get up).

> *Quelle heure est-il?*

> *Il est huit heures, Mademoiselle.*

> *Et maintenant?*

> *Il est neuf heures et quart.*

Quelle heure est-il?

To answer *Quelle heure est-il?* (What time is it?, What's the time?), you say *Il est...* (It is...):

une heure	one (o'clock)[2]
deux/trois heures	two/three (o'clock)
six heures (du matin)	six (in the morning)
...de l'après-midi	...in the afternoon
...du soir	...in the evening
midi/minuit	midday/midnight
deux heures et quart/demie	(a) quarter/half past two
deux heures moins le quart	(a) quarter to two
deux heures dix/vingt	ten/twenty past two
deux heures moins dix	ten to two

To answer *À quelle heure?* (What time? as in "What time's your train?") put *à* (at) in front of the time, for example *À une heure* (At one (o'clock)).

> *Gaston, à quelle heure est-ce que tu te lèves?*

> *À sept heures et demie.*

> *Est-ce que tu t'habilles tout seul?*

> *Bien sûr.*

> *Je ne me sens pas bien.*

> *Bon, calmez-vous!*

"Who" and "which"

English can use these words as a verb's subject ("The girl who/The book which is there...") or object ("The girl who(m)[3] I like...", "The book which I like..."). "Who(m)" refers to a person, "which" to a thing. However, we also often say "that" instead of "who(m)/which", or we drop the word altogether ("The book I like...").

French is simpler. Whether referring to a person or a thing, it uses *qui* for the subject, so you say *La fille/Le livre qui est là...* and *que* for the object: *La fille/Le livre que j'aime...* and *qui* or *que* are never left out. *Que* shortens to *qu'* before a vowel (and sometimes before an "h"), but *qui* never shortens.

> *Regarde! C'est le crayon qui manque.*

> *Hé! C'est mon dessin que tu déchires.*

---

24   **1** Many verbs are used either as a normal verb or as a reflexive, e.g. *casser* means "to break (something)", but *se casser* means "to break" as in "The cup broke". **2** Numbers are shown on page 58. **3** Note that "whom" is better English for the object.

Speech bubble key

- *Pourquoi est-ce que vous vous cachez?* Why are you hiding?
- *Parce qu'on n'aime pas l'école.* Because we don't like school.
- *Quelle heure est-il?* What's the time?
- *Il est huit heures, Mademoiselle.* It's eight o'clock, Miss.
- *Et maintenant?* And now?
- *Il est neuf heures et quart.* It's quarter past nine.
- *Gaston, à quelle heure est-ce que tu te lèves?* Gaston, what time do you get up?
- *À sept heures et demie.* At half past seven.
- *Est-ce que tu t'habilles tout seul?* Do you get dressed on your own?
- *Bien sûr.* Of course.
- *Je ne me sens pas bien.* I don't feel well.
- *Bon, calmez-vous!* Right, calm down!
- *Regarde! C'est le crayon qui manque.* Look! That's the crayon that's missing.
- *Hé! C'est mon dessin que tu déchires.* Hey! That's my drawing (which) you're tearing up.
- *Oh! Ce doit être l'indice que nous cherchons.* Oh! That must be the clue (that) we're looking for.
- *Regarde cette vieille photo.* Look at that old photo.
- *C'est Clément Camembert qui coupe le ruban.* That's Clément Camembert (who's) cutting the ribbon.
- *Et voilà le signe qui se trouve sur tous ses indices.* And there's the sign that's on all his clues.
- *On peut revenir ce soir.* We can come back this evening.
- *Bonne idée!* Good idea!

New words

la journée[4]	day	*se calmer*	to calm down
le livre	book	*manquer*	to be missing
le crayon (de couleur)	crayon	*déchirer*	to tear (up)
		couper	to cut
le dessin	drawing	*se trouver*	to be, to be found / situated
le ruban	ribbon		
le signe	sign	*(bien) s'amuser*	to have (lots of) fun
le soir	evening	*emprunter*	to borrow
l'idée [f]	idea	*se laver*	to have a wash, to get washed
la carte postale	postcard		
		se réveiller	to wake up
se raser	to shave	*se coucher*	to go to bed
se terminer	to end, to finish		
se cacher	to hide	*tout(e) seul(e)*	all alone
s'habiller	to dress, to get dressed	*bien sûr*	of course
se sentir bien / mal	to feel well / not well	*sympa(thique)*	nice
		(gros) baisers	(lots of) kisses

A postcard from Céline

While they wait for school to end so they can take a closer look at the old photo, Céline writes a postcard home. Read it and see if you can answer the questions. (Give full sentence answers in French.)

Chère Maman,

Nous nous amusons bien ici. La maison Camembert est très chouette et les parents de Marion sont sympas. Ils ont aussi un locataire sympa, Jean, un chien et un chat, et des voisins qui ont une chèvre. Il y a des bicyclettes que nous pouvons emprunter. Nous dormons dans les tentes (qui sont dans le jardin), mais on mange et on se lave dans la maison. Je me réveille à six heures du matin parce que le soleil brille et les oiseaux chantent, mais Luc se réveille à huit heures! On se couche à neuf heures et demie ou dix heures. Aimes-tu cette carte postale? Elle est de Port-le-Vieux.

Gros baisers, Céline

Madame
Annie Meun
7, rue des Capu
Paris 75013

Qui a une chèvre?
Où dorment Céline et Luc?
Où est-ce qu'ils mangent et se lavent?
À quelle heure est-ce que Céline se réveille?
À quelle heure est-ce que Luc se réveille?
À quelle heure est-ce qu'ils se couchent?

---

4 *Le jour* also means "day". You normally use *le jour* when you want to specify an amount of time, e.g. *trois jours* (three days).

Saying what you are doing

You already know that French just has one present tense where English has two (so that *Je fais* means "I do" or "I'm doing"). However you can stress that you are doing something right now (or "just doing" it) by using *être* + *en train de* (or *d'*) + an infinitive verb, for example *Je suis en train de manger* (I'm (just) eating).

Faire (to do, to make)

This is an irregular verb that is used in all sorts of everyday expressions:[1]

je fais	I do (am doing)
tu fais	you do
il/elle fait	he/she/it does
nous faisons	we do
vous faites	you do
ils/elles font	they do

Qui êtes-vous? Que faites-vous ici?

Euh . . . Je suis mécanicien.[2] Je suis en train de réparer la photocopieuse.

Alors, ça va maintenant?

Euh, oui . . .

Oui . . . Je suis en train d'emballer une pièce cassée.

Est-ce que je peux fermer, Monsieur Vial?

Oui, bien sûr.

Parce que and à cause de

Parce que means "because", for example *Je veux un nouveau pull parce que ce pull est moche* (I want a new jumper because this jumper's horrible). For "because of", you use *à cause de*, for instance *Je reste ici à cause de la pluie* (I'm staying here because of the rain). With *le* and *les*, *de* changes in the usual way to *du* and *des* (*À cause du soleil* – Because of the sun).

Pour (in order to, to)

Pour can mean "for" (see page 22), but is also used with a verb in the infinitive to mean "in order to", "so as to", "to", for example *Ils vont à l'école pour trouver un indice* (They go to the school to find a clue).

Qu'est-ce qu'on fait pour entrer?

Venez par ici!

Qu'est-ce que tu fais, Céline?

Ne sois pas bête . . .

Je cherche la photo parce qu'elle n'est plus sur le mur.

Trop tard! L'homme chauve a l'indice.

Comment tu sais ça?

Parce que c'est sa serviette.

Bon, on emporte ça à la gendarmerie.

Connaître (to know)

je connais	I know
tu connais	you know
il/elle connaît	he/she/it knows
nous connaissons	we know
vous connaissez	you know
ils/elles connaissent	they know

Savoir and connaître

The irregular verb *savoir* (see page 18) means "to know" in the sense of "know how to" or "know that . . .". For "to know" in the sense of "be acquainted with" (people, films, books and so on), French has a different verb, *connaître*. This is another irregular verb which is used very often, and its present tense is shown here. *Reconnaître* (to recognize) follows the same pattern.

---

1 E.g. *faire des courses* (to do some shopping). **2** When you use *être* and the name of a profession, you use the noun without the word for "a".

New words

le mécanicien	mechanic	cassé(e)	broken
la photocopieuse	photocopier	bien sûr	of course
la pièce	part, room	moche	horrible, ugly
la pluie	rain	bête	stupid, daft
la gendarmerie	police station	ne ... plus[3]	not any more, no longer
le gendarme	policeman		
		tard	late
réparer	to repair, to mend	ça, cela	this, that[4]
emballer	to wrap (up)	demain matin	tomorrow morning
fermer	to close, to shut	assez	quite
entrer	to go in, to enter	difficile	difficult
emporter	to take (away)		
reconnaître	to recognize		
travailler	to work		

Speech bubble key

- *Qui êtes-vous? Que faites-vous ici?* Who are you? What are you doing here?
- *Euh ... Je suis mécanicien.[2] Je suis en train de réparer la photocopieuse.* Er ... I'm a mechanic. I'm just mending the photocopier.
- *Oui ... Je suis en train d'emballer une pièce cassée.* Yes ... I'm just wrapping up a broken part.
- *Alors, ça va maintenant?* So, it's OK now?
- *Euh, oui ...* Er, yes ...
- *Est-ce que je peux fermer, Monsieur Vial?* Can I close up, Mr Vial?
- *Oui, bien sûr.* Yes, of course.
- *Qu'est-ce qu'on fait pour entrer?* What do we do to get in?
- *Venez par ici!* Come this way!
- *Qu'est-ce que tu fais, Céline?* What are you doing, Céline?
- *Ne sois pas bête ...* Don't be daft ...
- *Je cherche la photo parce qu'elle n'est plus sur le mur.* I'm looking for the photo because it's not on the wall any more.
- *Trop tard! L'homme chauve a l'indice.* Too late! The bald man's got the clue.
- *Comment tu sais ça?* How do you know?
- *Parce que c'est sa serviette.* Because that's his briefcase.
- *Bon, on emporte ça à la gendarmerie.* Right, we're taking this to the police station.
- *C'est fermé!* It's closed!
- *Bon, il faut revenir demain matin.* Right, we must come back tomorrow morning.
- *Est-ce que tu connais le gendarme?* Do you know the policeman?
- *Oui ... Il est assez sympa.* Yes ... He's quite nice.

Mix and match

Here are two sets of six sentences. Each sentence from the first set can be joined to one from the second set using *parce que* or *pour*. Can you work out what the six new sentences are? (You should use *pour* in the two cases where it is possible. When you do, you must drop the first two words from the second sentence.)

Nous ne pouvons pas venir maintenant.
Je prends ta bicyclette.
Nous connaissons Madame Cachet.
Tais-toi! Je dois réfléchir.
Elle va à Tourville.
Le mécanicien est ici.

Elle veut faire des courses.
C'est très difficile.
Je veux aller à Port-le-Vieux.
Elle travaille à la pharmacie.
La machine est cassée.
Nous sommes en train de manger.

3 This works like *ne ... rien* (see page 18). **4** *Ça* is short for *cela*, meaning "this/that (thing)" or "it". Unlike *ce, cette* (see page 12), *ça/cela* is used instead of a noun rather than in front of one.

Personal pronouns

Personal pronouns are words like "I", "you" and so on. When they are the object of a verb, some of them change, for example "I" becomes "me". In English, the word is the same for a direct or an indirect object: you say "He watches me" and "He passes the book to me" (or "passes me the book"). In French, the pronoun may have different forms (see right).

subject	direct object	indirect object
je/j' (I)	*me/m'* (me)	*me/m'* ((to)[1] me)
tu (you)	*te/t'* (you)	*te/t'* ((to) you)
il (he/it)	*le/l'* (him/it)	*lui* ((to) him/it)
elle (she/it)	*la/l'* (her/it)	*lui* ((to) her/it)
nous (we)	*nous* (us)	*nous* ((to) us)
vous (you)	*vous* (you)	*vous* ((to) you)
ils (they)	*les* (them)	*leur* ((to) them)
elles (they)	*les* (them)	*leur* ((to) them)

Word order

French personal pronouns always go before the verb (except in a few cases, such as with a verb in the imperative), for example *Il me regarde* (He watches me). If you use two or more, they follow a set order which you should learn. This chart sums up the order they go in:

1	2	3
me	le	lui
te	la	leur
nous	les	
vous		

For example *Il me les donne* (He gives them to me) or *Il la lui donne* (He gives it to her).

Personal pronouns with imperatives

In French, if you need to use a personal pronoun with an imperative (see page 14), you use the object personal pronouns listed at the top, except you say *moi* and *toi* instead of *me* and *te*, for example *Passe-moi* (or *Passez-moi*) *le livre* (Pass me the book) or *Passe-le moi* (Pass it to me). Notice that there is a hyphen after the verb.

A mixed set

In a few cases, French uses a set of personal pronouns that is not quite the same as any of those in the chart above. It is: *moi, toi, lui, elle, nous, vous, eux, elles.*

This set is used: 1) after prepositions; 2) after *c'est*; 3) in short answers, e.g. *Qui est là? Moi!* (Who's there? Me!) and in exclamations.

1 The French indirect pronoun already means "to me/you, etc." so to say things like "He passes the book to me", you don't translate "to" separately.

The postcard jigsaw

Here are the pieces of postcard that Luc, Céline and Marion have to put together. Try writing it out with all the bits in the right order, and then work out the meaning of the postcard in English.

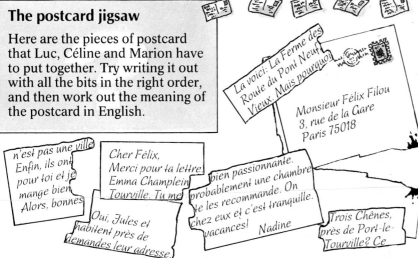

Speech bubble key

- *Qu'est-ce qu'on fait avec la serviette?* What do we do with the briefcase?
- *Est-ce qu'on la montre à tes parents?* Do we show it to your parents?
- *Non, on ne doit pas la leur montrer . . .* No, we mustn't show it to them . . .
- *On doit d'abord tout raconter à la police.* We must first tell the police everything.
- *On dîne!* We're eating!
- *Je peux la cacher dans ma tente.* I can hide it in my tent.
- *Bonne idée.* Good idea.
- *L'homme chauve a l'indice de l'école.* The bald man's got the clue from the school.
- *Pour le trouver, il faut trouver l'homme chauve.* To find it, we have to find the bald man.
- *Son adresse est peut-être dans sa serviette.* His address might be[2] in his briefcase.
- *Viens à côté de moi.* You come next to me.
- *Céline, passe-lui ma lampe.* Céline, pass her my torch.
- *Un agenda, un journal . . .* A diary, a newspaper . . .
- *Mais regarde en dessous, il y a des bouts de papier.* But look underneath, there are some bits of paper.
- *Qu'est-ce que c'est?* What's that?
- *Ah, c'est toi, Minou!* Oh, it's you, Minou!
- *C'est une carte postale en petits morceaux.* It's a postcard in small pieces.
- *Mais est-ce qu'on peut la lire?* But can we read it?

New words

la police	the police	montrer	to show	peut-être	maybe, perhaps
l'adresse [f]	address	raconter	to tell	en dessous	underneath
la lampe (de poche)	torch, flashlight	cacher	to hide	enfin	at last, anyhow
		passer	to pass, to hand	probablement	probably
l'agenda [m]	diary	lire*	to read	chez moi/toi, etc.	at my/your, etc. place
le journal	newspaper	demander	to ask		
le bout	bit, piece	recommander	to recommend	bonnes vacances!	(have a) good holiday/ vacation!
le papier	paper				
le morceau(x)	piece	tout	everything		

---

2 A verb + *peut-être* is often translated as "might be" instead of "is perhaps".

29

Past tenses and adverbs

So far, you have learned verbs in the present tense. From here to page 39, you will learn about past tenses. These are for talking about what happened in the past, for example in English "She did her homework", "She was doing her homework", "She has done her homework". You can see that English has many past tenses. So has French – one of these past tenses is called the imperfect.

The imperfect tense of *avoir* and *être*

The two most useful verbs to learn in the imperfect tense are *avoir* and *être*. For them, the imperfect is the most commonly used past tense.

Avoir (imperfect tense)	
j'avais	I had
tu avais	you had
il/elle avait	he/she/it had
nous avions	we had
vous aviez	you had
ils/elles avaient	they had

Être (imperfect tense)	
j'étais	I was
tu étais	you were
il/elle était	he/she/it was
nous étions	we were
vous étiez	you were
ils/elles étaient	they were

The next morning . . .

Alors, où était cette serviette?

Elle était sur la photocopieuse de l'école.

Et pourquoi étiez-vous là?

Parce que nous cherchons un trésor . . .

et il y avait[1] un indice dans l'école.

Quel trésor?

Il appartient à ma famille.

Ah, je comprends, et cet escroc veut le voler . . .

Adverbs

These are words like "slowly" or "nicely" that give extra meaning to a verb. There are various types, for instance adverbs of time (that say when something happens), or of place (where it happens), or of manner (how it happens). French adverbs of manner are easy to spot as many end in *-ment*. They are made by adding *-ment* to an adjective – so *vrai* (true, real) becomes *vraiment* (really).[2]

Exactement! L'indice est une vieille photo.

Hier soir la photo n'était plus là . . .

mais il y avait la serviette de l'escroc.

Elle est très probablement à l'instituteur.

Mais non, l'escroc l'avait avant.

Ça suffit! Rentrez chez vous maintenant.

Useful adverbs

Time

aujourd'hui	today
hier	yesterday
hier soir	yesterday evening, last night
avant-hier	the day before yesterday
demain	tomorrow
après-demain	the day after tomorrow
déjà	already
toujours	always, still
souvent	often
parfois, de temps en temps	sometimes
d'habitude	usually, normally
alors	then, so, well

Place

ici	here
là(-bas)	(over) there
par ici	over/around here
partout	everywhere
quelque part	somewhere
nulle part	nowhere

Manner

heureusement	luckily, happily, fortunately
probablement	probably
exactement	exactly
vraiment	really
très	very
peut-être	maybe
presque	almost, nearly

30 1 The expression *il y a* is made with *avoir*, so in the imperfect tense you say *il y avait*. 2 Useful exceptions are *bien* (well), *mal* (badly) and *fort* (loudly). Note that the *-ment* ending is added to the feminine form of most adjectives that end in a consonant, e.g. *lentement* (slowly).

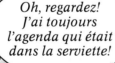

Rapportez vite cette serviette à l'école.

Tant pis! Il faut continuer sans la police.

Heureusement, on connaît l'adresse de l'homme chauve.

Oh, regardez! J'ai toujours l'agenda qui était dans la serviette!

Il était dans ma poche.

New words

la famille	family	rentrer	to come/go (back/home)
l'escroc [m]	crook	rapporter	to bring/take back
l'instituteur [m]	(junior school) teacher	tant pis	too bad
la poche	pocket	petit(e)	small, short
le restaurant	restaurant	joli(e)	pretty
voler	to steal, to rob	cher (chère)	expensive

Picture puzzle

The girl in the pink shirt is showing her friend her holiday photos. Can you match the six things she says with the right photos?

1 *Notre hôtel était petit et sympa.*
2 *Il y avait un grand jardin.*
3 *La plage était tout près de l'hôtel.*
4 *J'avais une très jolie chambre.*
5 *Mes parents étaient vraiment fatigués.*
6 *Les restaurants n'étaient pas très chers.*

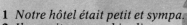
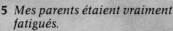

Speech bubble key

- *Alors, où était cette serviette?* So, where was this briefcase?
- *Elle était sur la photocopieuse de l'école.* It was on the school photocopier.
- *Et pourquoi étiez-vous là?* And why were you there?
- *Parce que nous cherchons un trésor . . .* Because we're looking for treasure . . .
- *et il y avait un indice dans l'école.* and there was a clue in the school.
- *Quel trésor?* What treasure?
- *Il appartient à ma famille.* It belongs to my family.
- *Ah, je comprends, et cet escroc veut le voler . . .* Ah, I see, and this crook wants to steal it . . .
- *Exactement! L'indice est une vieille photo.* Exactly! The clue is an old photo.
- *Hier soir la photo n'était plus là . . .* The photo wasn't there any more last night . . .
- *mais il y avait la serviette de l'escroc.* but the crook's briefcase was there.
- *Elle est très probablement à l'instituteur.* It's very probably the teacher's.
- *Mais non, l'escroc l'avait avant.* But no, the crook had it before.
- *Ça suffit! Rentrez chez vous maintenant.* That's enough! Go home now.
- *Rapportez vite cette serviette à l'école.* Quickly take this briefcase back to the school.
- *Tant pis! Il faut continuer sans la police.* Too bad! We must carry on without the police.
- *Heureusement, on connaît l'adresse de l'homme chauve.* Luckily, we know the bald man's address.
- *Oh, regardez! J'ai toujours l'agenda qui était dans la serviette!* Oh look! I've still got the diary that was in the briefcase!
- *Il était dans ma poche.* It was in my pocket.

The imperfect tense

The French imperfect tense has two uses. It is used for things that were happening – where, for example, you would say "I was cycling". It is also used for things that used to happen often, such as "I cycled to school every day". Note that English can say the same thing (I cycled) for things that happened often and for a one-off past event – "I cycled to school every day" and "I cycled to school that day" – but French uses different tenses, the imperfect for things that happened often, and the perfect for one-off past events (see page 34).

How to form the imperfect tense

French verbs all form the imperfect tense from the present tense *nous* form.[1] You drop the ending (*-ons*) and add a set of imperfect endings, as shown here by the imperfect of *choisir* (present tense *nous* form: *nous choisissons*):

je choisissais	I was choosing/chose (often)
tu choisissais	you were choosing
il/elle choisissait	he/she/it was choosing
nous choisissions	we were choosing
vous choisissiez	you were choosing
ils/elles choisissaient	they were choosing

Y and more about *il y a*

Y is a useful word meaning "there", as in *La gare? J'y étais hier* (The station? I was there yesterday). You use it when the place it refers to is already clear. As the example shows, it comes before the verb.

As you know, *y* is used in the expression *il y a* (there is/are). *Il y a* can also mean "ago", as in *Il y a un an* (A year ago).

En

When English uses "some" or "any" on their own, as in "I'd like some" or "I don't want any", French uses *en*: *J'en veux* or *Je n'en veux pas*. *En* comes before the verb, and after *y* if you use both (*Il y en a* – There is/are some). For amounts, you often use *en* where English might not have a word at all, for example *Des pommes? J'en veux deux kilos* (Apples? I want two kilos (of them)).

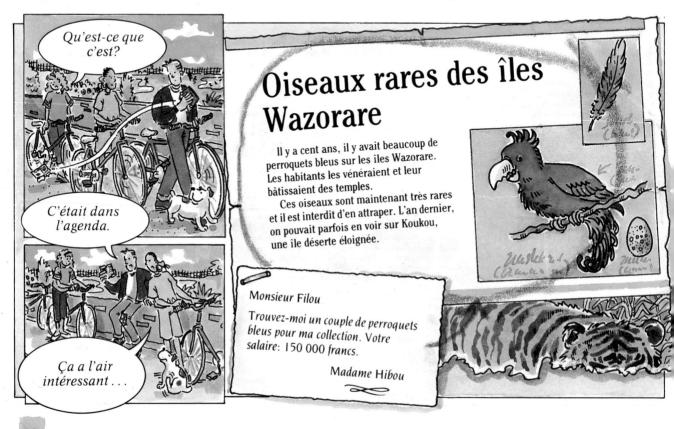

Qu'est-ce que c'est?

C'était dans l'agenda.

Ça a l'air intéressant . . .

Oiseaux rares des îles Wazorare

Il y a cent ans, il y avait beaucoup de perroquets bleus sur les îles Wazorare. Les habitants les vénéraient et leur bâtissaient des temples.

Ces oiseaux sont maintenant très rares et il est interdit d'en attraper. L'an dernier, on pouvait parfois en voir sur Koukou, une île déserte éloignée.

Monsieur Filou

Trouvez-moi un couple de perroquets bleus pour ma collection. Votre salaire: 150 000 francs.

Madame Hibou

32   1 The only exception is *être*. Its imperfect is not formed from *nous sommes*, as you can see on page 30.

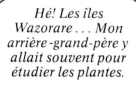

> *Hé! Les îles Wazorare... Mon arrière-grand-père y allait souvent pour étudier les plantes.*

> *Il était botaniste...*

> *Et l'homme chauve était dans ces îles pour voler des perroquets.*

> *Venez, je veux vous montrer quelque chose à la maison.*

Speech bubble key

- *Qu'est-ce que c'est?* What's that?
- *C'était dans l'agenda.* It was in the diary.
- *Ça a l'air intéressant...* It looks interesting...

- **The magazine cutting:** Rare birds on the Wazorare islands
A hundred years ago, there were many blue parrots on the Wazorare islands. The inhabitants worshipped them and built temples to them. These birds are now very rare and it is forbidden to catch any. Last year, you could sometimes see some on Koukou, a remote desert island.

- **The message:** Mr Filou Find me a pair of blue parrots for my collection. Your fee: 150,000 francs. Mrs Hibou

- *Hé! Les îles Wazorare... Mon arrière-grand-père y allait souvent pour étudier les plantes.* Hey! The Wazorare islands... My great-grandfather often went there to study the plants.
- *Il était botaniste...* He was a botanist...
- *Et l'homme chauve était dans ces îles pour voler des perroquets.* And the bald man was on those islands to steal some parrots.
- *Venez, je veux vous montrer quelque chose à la maison.* Come on, I want to show you something at home.

New words

l'an [m], *l'année* [f]	year
le perroquet	parrot
l'habitant [m]	inhabitant
le temple	temple
le couple	couple, pair
la collection	collection
le salaire	pay, salary, fee
le franc	franc[2]
la plante	plant
le botaniste	botanist
la disparition	disappearance
la saison des tempêtes	stormy season
le gouverneur	governor
avoir l'air	to look, to seem, to appear
vénérer	to worship
bâtir	to build
il est interdit de/d'	it is forbidden to
attraper	to catch
voir*	to see
étudier	to study
intéressant(e)	interesting
rare	rare
cent	a hundred
beaucoup de	many, a lot of
dernier (dernière)	last
éloigné(e)	remote, far-away
quelque chose	something
malheureusement	unfortunately, sadly
mort(e)	dead
lors de	at the time of
dangereux (dangereuse)	dangerous

Clément Camembert's disappearance

Back at home, Marion shows her friends an old letter addressed to her grandfather, Joseph. To find out what it says, read it and translate it into English.

> *Wazorareville*
>
> *Monsieur,*
> *Malheureusement, votre père est très probablement mort. Il connaissait bien nos îles, mais lors de sa disparition, il cherchait des plantes sur des îles dangereuses et très éloignées. Il était avec deux amis botanistes. Ils avaient un bon bateau, mais c'était la saison des tempêtes.*
>
> *Pedro Paté*
> *Gouverneur des îles*

2 This is French money.

33

The perfect tense

French uses the perfect tense to talk about once-only events that happened in the past (such as "I saw Rob yesterday"), as opposed to events that were happening or used to happen regularly. For example, in "I was reading when I heard the alarm. I rang the police . . .", the first verb (was reading) would be in the imperfect, and the others (heard, rang) in the perfect.

How to form the perfect tense

The perfect tense is made of two bits – the present tense of *avoir* (or sometimes *être*) plus a special form of the verb you are using, called the past participle. For example, the perfect tense *je* form of *marcher* is *j'ai marché* (I walked). The few verbs that form the perfect with *être* are shown on page 36.

The past participle

The past participle of regular verbs is easy to form. "Er" verbs add "é" to their stem[1] (as shown above with *marché*) and most "ir" verbs add "i" (for example, *choisir*, *choisi*, and *partir*, *parti*). For irregular verbs, you have to learn the past participle. A few are shown below – they all form the perfect with *avoir*, for example, *J'ai eu* (I had).

Useful irregular participles

avoir, eu	*perdre, perdu*
attendre, attendu	*prendre, pris*
connaître, connu	*pouvoir, pu*
devoir, dû	*savoir, su*
être, été	*voir, vu*
faire, fait	*vouloir, voulu*
mettre, mis	

Agreement of the participle

When you use a perfect tense made with *avoir*, if you put a direct object before the verb, the past participle agrees with it like an adjective (see page 8). For example, talking about a key (*la clé* – feminine), you might say *Je l'ai trouvée* (I found it).

Le déjeuner est presque prêt.

Est-ce que tu as rapporté du pain?

Oh pardon, j'ai oublié!

Ça ne fait rien.

Il faut attendre Papa . . . Il arrive bientôt.

Est-ce que tu as l'agenda?

Marion, les bicyclettes! Il pleut . . .

Non, je l'ai mis dans ma tente. Attendez ici!

Ça va, on les a rangées.

New words

le déjeuner	lunch	*attendre**	to wait	*prêt(e)*	ready
le pain	bread	*mettre**	to put	*ça ne fait rien*	it doesn't
l'entrée [f]	entrance	*oublier*	to forget		matter
la grotte	cave	*il pleut*	it rains/is raining	*Papa*	Dad, Daddy
le coffre	chest (container)	*ranger*	to put away	*bientôt*	soon
la réunion	meeting	*expliquer*	to explain	*rouillé(e)*	rusty
la clé	key	*réussir (à)*	to manage (to), to	*dedans*	inside
la poche	pocket		succeed (in)	*long(ue)*	long
le propriétaire	owner, landlord	*atteindre**	to reach, to get to	*comme*	as (a/the)
le coffre-fort	safe	*parler*	to talk, to speak		
la récompense	reward	*perdre**	to lose		

1 The stem of "er" and "ir" verbs is the infinitive minus "er" or "ir".

Telling a story

Try telling this story using all the right tenses. You will have to put two verbs into the imperfect and six into the perfect.

Deux copains, Fred et Loïc, (faire) des courses. Ils (chercher) des jeans. Dans un magasin, ils (trouver) des clés dans la poche d'un jean. Ils les (donner) au propriétaire. "Les clés de mon coffre-fort! Merci! Je les (perdre) hier. Je les (chercher) partout, mais je ne les pas (trouver)." Comme récompense, il leur (donner) des jeans.

Speech bubble key

- *Le déjeuner est presque prêt.* Lunch is nearly ready.
- *Est-ce que tu as rapporté du pain?* Did you bring back any bread?
- *Oh pardon, j'ai oublié!* Oh sorry, I forgot!
- *Ça ne fait rien.* It doesn't matter.
- *Il faut attendre Papa . . . Il arrive bientôt.* We have to wait for Dad . . . He's on his way ("He's coming soon").
- *Marion, les bicyclettes! Il pleut . . .* Marion, the bicycles! It's raining . . .
- *Ça va, on les a rangées.* It's OK, we put them away.
- *Est-ce que tu as l'agenda?* Have you got the diary?
- *Non, je l'ai mis dans ma tente. Attendez ici!* No, I put it in my tent. Wait here!
- *Oh . . . Il explique comment il a trouvé la lettre de Clément Camembert.* Oh . . . He explains how he found Clément Camembert's letter.
- *Il cherchait des perroquets bleus.* He was looking for blue parrots.
- *Il a réussi à atteindre l'île Koukou . . .* He managed to get to Koukou island . . .
- *À l'entrée d'une grotte, il a vu un vieux coffre rouillé.* At the entrance to a cave, he saw an old rusty chest.
- *Dedans il a trouvé une lettre qui parlait de trésor.* Inside he found a letter that talked about treasure.
- *Oui, la lettre qu'il a volée . . .* Yes, the letter that he stole . . .
- *À table! Voici Papa.* Come to the table! Here's Dad.
- *Pardon, mais j'ai eu une très longue réunion . . .* Sorry, but I had a very long meeting . . .

The perfect tense with *être*

The perfect tense of certain verbs is formed with the present tense of *être*, not *avoir*, for example *Je suis arrivé* (I arrived). There are two types of verbs that work like this: firstly, a small number of verbs that can be called "*être* verbs" (see below), and secondly, all reflexive verbs.

Être verbs

Here are the most useful *être* verbs. Notice that most of these verbs involve either a change of place or of state, for example *aller* (to go) or *mourir* (to die). The past participles of irregular verbs are shown in brackets.

aller (allé)	to go	*monter*	to go up(stairs)
venir (venu)	to come	*descendre (descendu)*	to go down(stairs)
revenir (revenu)	to come back	*naître (né)*	to be born
devenir (devenu)	to become	*mourir (mort)*	to die
arriver	to arrive	*tomber*	to fall (over)
partir	to leave	*rester*	to stay
retourner	to go back		
entrer	to come in		
rentrer	to go home		
sortir	to go out		

Il faut aller à la ferme des Trois Chênes...

pour retrouver Monsieur Filou et l'indice de l'école.

Du café, Monsieur Filou?

Merci... Euh, je voulais vous demander...

Je suis allé à Tourville ce matin.

J'ai vu le château et les deux tours...

mais je n'ai pas trouvé la tour en ruine.

Pourquoi voulez-vous la voir? Il y a seulement quelques vieilles pierres.

Euh... j'aime les ruines...

Eh bien, êtes-vous allé au jardin public?

Oui, mais je n'y ai rien vu.

Ah! Vous n'êtes pas descendu jusqu'à la rivière...

🗨 Speech bubble key

●*Il faut aller à la ferme des Trois Chênes...* We must go to Trois Chênes farm...
●*pour retrouver Monsieur Filou et l'indice de l'école.* to find Mr Filou and the clue from the school.
●*Du café, Monsieur Filou?* Some coffee, Mr Filou?
●*Merci... Euh, je voulais vous demander...* Thank you... Er, I wanted to ask you...
●*Je suis allé à Tourville ce matin.* I went to Tourville this morning.
●*J'ai vu le château et les deux tours...* I saw the castle and the two towers...
●*mais je n'ai pas trouvé la tour en ruine.* but I didn't find the ruined tower.
●*Pourquoi voulez-vous la voir? Il y a seulement quelques vieilles pierres.* Why do you want to see it? There's only a few old stones.
●*Euh... j'aime les ruines...* Er... I like ruins...
●*Eh bien, êtes-vous allé au jardin public?* Well, did you go to the park?

36 1 Remember that with *avoir* verbs, you only have an agreement if the verb has a direct object before it (see page 34). 2 If a plural subject is a mixture of feminine and masculine, the agreement is masculine plural. 3 There is an exception to this. A few

Agreement of the past participle

For *être* verbs, the past participle agrees with the subject,[1] so for example if a girl is talking, an "e" is added to the past participle (*je suis arrivée*), or in the *nous* form, you either add a plural "s" or a feminine plural "es" (*nous sommes arrivé(e)s*), and so on.[2]

This rule also applies for reflexive verbs, for example *elle s'est lavée* (she had a wash).[3]

New words

la pierre	stone, rock
la ruine	ruin
le jardin public	park
le veau(x)	calf
la fenêtre	window
retrouver	to find (again), to track down
ce matin	this morning
en ruine	ruined, in ruins
seulement	only
quelques	a few
beau (belle)[4]	beautiful, good-looking
au bord de	by (the side of)

Oui, Marguerite a eu un beau veau hier soir.

Je me suis couchée à deux heures du matin!

Oui, ils vont bien.

Je suis allée les voir ce matin.

...Oui, la tour en ruine est au bord de la rivière.

Le prochain indice doit être à la vieille tour.

Ah bon... C'est très intéressant.

Say it in French

Put these sentences into French. The verbs must go into the perfect tense, but some form the perfect with *avoir* and some with *être*.

Monsieur Filou looked for the ruined tower, but he didn't find it.
Céline, Luc and Marion went to the farm.
They found Monsieur Filou.
He didn't see them.
Céline and Marion hid under the window.

- *Oui, mais je n'y ai rien vu.* Yes, but I didn't see anything there.
- *Ah! Vous n'êtes pas descendu jusqu'à la rivière...* Ah! You didn't go down to the river.
- *Oui, Marguerite a eu un beau veau hier soir.* Yes, Marguerite had a lovely calf last night.
- *Je me suis couchée à deux heures du matin!* I went to bed at two o'clock in the morning!
- *Oui, ils vont bien.* Yes, they're well.
- *Je suis allée les voir ce matin.* I went to see them this morning.
- *...Oui, la tour en ruine est au bord de la rivière.* ...Yes, the ruined tower is by the river.
- *Ah bon... C'est très intéressant.* Oh really... That's very interesting.
- *Le prochain indice doit être à la vieille tour.* The next clue must be at the old tower.

reflexive verbs are often used with a direct object, and there is no agreement if the object follows the verb, e.g. *elle s'est lavé les mains* (she washed her hands). **4** The masculine form is *bel* before a vowel or "h".

More about the perfect tense

Like French, English has a perfect tense. This is made from "to have" and the past participle, for example "He has heard (that song)". Normally, where you use the perfect in English, you also use it in French, so you say *Il a entendu (cette chanson)*.

As you can see, French does not usually make the difference between "he heard" (see page 34) and "he has heard" – in either case, it uses the perfect (*il a entendu*).

More about the past participle

In English, the past participle can be used on its own like an adjective, for example "stolen goods". French can do the same thing, but the participle then behaves exactly like an adjective – it comes after the noun it is used with and agrees with it (see page 8), for example *des objets volés* (stolen goods).

"Mine", "yours", "his", etc.

There are two ways to say "mine", "yours" and so on. With *être*, you mostly use the same method as for saying "It's Luc's" (*Il est à Luc* – see page 12). You say *à moi* (mine), *à toi* (yours), *à lui* (his, its), *à elle* (hers, its), *à nous* (ours), *à vous* (yours), or *à eux/elles* (theirs – m/f), for example *C'est à moi* (It's mine).

Otherwise, you use a special set of words (see right). These change to match the noun they are replacing, for example, talking about a suitcase (*une valise*), you say *La mienne est bleue* (Mine is blue).

(m)	(f)	(m pl)	(f pl)	
le mien	la mienne	les miens	les miennes	mine
le tien	la tienne	les tiens	les tiennes	yours
le sien	la sienne	les siens	les siennes	hers/ his/its
le nôtre	la nôtre	les nôtres	les nôtres	ours
le vôtre	la vôtre	les vôtres	les vôtres	yours
le leur	la leur	les leurs	les leurs	theirs

New words

la chanson	song
l'objet [m]	object, thing
l'oreille [f]	ear
la clôture	fence
la casquette	cap
le monument	monument
le pirate	pirate
la bataille	battle
le fort	fort
le pays	country
*entendre** (past participle: *entendu*)	to hear
déchiffrer	to decipher, to work out
*envoyer**	to send
*avoir** besoin de*	to need
casser	to break

explorer	to explore
examiner	to examine
garder	to keep
*détruire** (past participle: *détruit*)	to destroy
se venger	to get your revenge
gagner	to win, to earn
chasser	to chase (away), to expel
*disparaître** (past participle: *disparu*)	to disappear
ne... pas encore[2]	not yet
donc	so, therefore
chaque	each
sacré(e)	sacred

The writing on the tower

Clément Camembert put his sign on an old plaque. This is what Luc, Céline and Marion see when they clear away the ivy. It gives them a good idea of where to go next. Translate it and see what you think.

> Nous avons gardé cette tour en ruine parce que c'est un monument sacré pour les habitants de Tourville.
>
> Les pirates de l'île des Pirates l'ont détruite il y a trois ans, mais maintenant, nous nous sommes vengés. Nous avons gagné notre dernière bataille contre eux, nous les avons chassés de leur fort sur l'île et ils ont disparu de notre pays.

Speech bubble key

- *Alors, il a déchiffré l'indice de l'école...* So, he's worked out the clue from the school...
- *qui l'a envoyé à la tour en ruine.* which sent him to the ruined tower.
- *Mais il ne l'a pas encore trouvée.* But he hasn't found it yet.
- *Donc nous devons y aller tout de suite – avant lui.* So we must go there straight away – before him.
- *On est revenu parce qu'on a besoin des bicyclettes.* We've come back because we need the bikes.
- *Bonjour, Madame. Pouvez-vous réparer cette oreille cassée?* Hello. Can you mend this broken ear?
- *Je n'ai jamais vraiment exploré la tour à cause de la clôture.* I've never really explored the tower because of the fence.
- *À qui est cette casquette?* Whose cap is this?
- *À lui!* It's his!
- *Mais non, il a la sienne.* No it's not, he's got his.
- *Regarde, tu n'as plus la tienne!* Look, you haven't got yours anymore.
- *Ah, c'est vrai...* Oh, that's true...
- *Rien! J'ai regardé partout et examiné chaque pierre.* Nothing! I've looked everywhere and examined each stone.
- *Eh, j'ai trouvé quelque chose ici!* Hey, I've found something here!
- *Regardez!... C'est le signe de Clément Camembert!* Look!... It's Clément Camembert's sign!

---

1 When using two verbs in the perfect tense with the same form of *avoir* or *être* (e.g. *J'ai regardé et j'ai examiné...*), you don't have to repeat the *avoir* or *être* part (you say *J'ai regardé et examiné*). **2** This works like *ne ... rien* (see page 18).

The future tense

Just as English, French has a future tense for talking about events in the future. This is usually used where English uses its future tense (We will/We'll walk).

How to form the future tense

The French future tense is easy to form. For most verbs, you take the infinitive and add these future endings: -ai, -as, -a, -ons, -ez, -ont (see the future tense of *marcher* below).

Verbs ending in "re" are exceptions to this rule. They lose the "e" before adding the future endings, for example *je prendrai* (I'll take). There are also a few verbs that do not use the infinitive to form the future, but have their own future stem instead. The most useful of these are shown below (just the *je* form, but this is enough to show the future stem that you add the endings to).

Marcher (future tense)

je marcherai	I will walk
tu marcheras	you will walk
il/elle marchera	he/she/it will walk
nous marcherons	we will walk
vous marcherez	you will walk
ils/elles marcheront	they will walk

Future tenses to learn

j'aurai (from *avoir*)	I'll have	je devrai (from *devoir*)	I'll have to
je serai (from *être*)	I'll be	je viendrai (from *venir*)	I'll come
j'irai (from *aller*)	I'll go	je voudrai (from *vouloir*)	I'll want
je ferai (from *faire*)	I'll do	je verrai (from *voir*)	I'll see
je saurai (from *savoir*)	I'll know		
je pourrai (from *pouvoir*)	I'll be able to	Note: the future of *il faut* is *il faudra*.	

New words

la traversée	crossing
la nuit	night
la feuille	leaf, sheet (of paper)
la piste	trail, piste
la direction	direction
l'endroit [m]	place
la terre	earth, soil
le piège	trap
la tâche	task
le barreau(x)	bar (on window)
le mur	wall
le panneau(x)	panel
le bois	wood
le bijou(x)	piece of jewellery
la fortune	fortune
faire* nuit[2]	to be night-time/dark
laisser	to leave (behind)
déranger	to disturb
salir	to dirty
s'inquiéter	to worry
dessiner	to draw
tomber dans le piège	to fall in the trap, to fall for it
dangereux (dangereuse)	dangerous
pendant	during
faux (fausse)	false
génial(e)	brilliant
mauvais(e)	wrong, bad
certainement	certainly, definitely
par là	that way, around/over there
à l'intérieur	inside

Alors, il faut aller à l'île des Pirates.

Il fera nuit et la traversée sera dangereuse.

Pas[1] aujourd'hui. On arrivera trop tard...

Mais l'homme trouvera l'indice ici et...

Eh bien, il faut cacher cet indice avec des feuilles. Voilà!

il ira peut-être à l'île pendant la nuit.

On peut aussi laisser une fausse piste.

Génial! Il partira dans la mauvaise direction...

et ne nous dérangera pas.

40 1 *Pas* can be used without *ne* to mean "not" when there is no verb. 2 You often use *faire* in the *il* form in expressions about the time of day, the weather etc, e.g. *Il fait beau* (It is fine).

The false trail

This is Marion's note. She has used funny writing. To discover where she is sending the bald man, you will have to work out how to read it. Then you can translate it into English.

C.C. ueiдA. àl tnores enutrof am te xuojib sem suoT. siob ne xuaennap sed ceva rum nu sarevuort ut, rueirétni'l À. àl rap sarertne uT. xuaerrab snas ertênef enu sarrev uT. xueiV-el-troP ed eiremradneg al à rella arduaf lI. eliciffid ares ellE. ehcât erèinred at icioV. séssial ia'j euq secidni sel suot évuort sa ut tnanetniaM, slif noM.

💬 Speech bubble key

- *Alors, il faut aller à l'île des Pirates.* So, we must go to Pirates' Island.
- *Pas aujourd'hui. On arrivera trop tard . . .* Not today. We'll get there too late . . .
- *Il fera nuit et la traversée sera dangereuse.* It'll be night-time and the crossing will be dangerous.
- *Mais l'homme trouvera l'indice ici et . . .* But the man will find the clue here and . . .
- *il ira peut-être à l'île pendant la nuit.* he might go to the island during the night.
- *Eh bien, il faut cacher cet indice avec des feuilles. Voilà!* Well, we must hide this clue with leaves. There!
- *On peut aussi laisser une fausse piste.* We can also leave a false trail.
- *Génial! Il partira dans la mauvaise direction . . .* Brilliant! He'll go off in the wrong direction . . .
- *et ne nous dérangera pas.* and won't[3] disturb us.
- *Bon, il faut lui laisser un mot.* Right, we must leave him a note.
- *J'ai une bonne idée.* I've got a good idea.
- *Mais où est-ce qu'on le cachera?* But where shall[4] we hide it?
- *On peut chercher un bon endroit, Luc et moi.* Luc and I can look for a good place.
- *Il faudra salir le mot avec de la terre.* You'll have to dirty the note with some soil.
- *Oui . . . Ne t'inquiète pas, il sera parfait.* Yes . . . Don't worry, it'll be perfect.
- *On peut le cacher ici et dessiner son signe!* We can hide it here and draw his sign!
- *C'est vraiment génial! Il tombera certainement dans le piège.* That's really brilliant! He's bound to (He'll definitely) fall for it.

---

3 Note that "will not" turns into "won't". **4** "Shall" can be used in English instead of "will" in the "I" and "we" forms, especially in questions.

More about the future

Apart from the future tense, French has another way of talking about the future. You can use the present tense of *aller* (to go – see page 22) plus the infinitive of the verb you need. This works exactly like the English "going to" future, for example *Je vais ouvrir la porte* (I'm going to open the door). [1]

Just as in English, the "going to" method often replaces the future tense in everyday French. As a general rule, use it whenever English might, but bear in mind that it is even more common in French, especially for events that are just about to happen.

The present tense used for the future

Sometimes both English and French use the present tense when talking about a future event, for example *Je pars demain matin* (I'm leaving tomorrow morning). On the whole, this is most common when you are using time words like "tomorrow" or "at one o'clock".

However, with words like *quand* (when) or *dès que* (as soon as), French uses the future tense whereas English uses the present, for example *Quand il arrivera, nous partirons* (When he gets here, we'll leave).

"This one", "that one"

The French words for "this one" and "that one" are *celui-ci* and *celui-là* in the masculine singular, and *celle-ci* or *celle-là* in the feminine. The plural forms ("these (ones)" and "those (ones)") are *ceux-ci* or *ceux-là* (masculine) and *celles-ci* or *celles-là* (feminine).

1 Note that although in English you can also use "will go and" (I'll go and open the door), you cannot do this in French.

New words

l'enfant [m]	child	*arrêter*	to stop, to arrest
le détail	detail		
le numéro	number	*quand*	when
la vitre	window pane	*dès que/qu'*	as soon as
le vol	theft	*X ans*	X years old
ouvrir*	to open	*recherché(e)*	sought after, wanted
mettre* *de l'ordre*	to tidy up		
faxer	to fax, to send a fax	*content(e)*	pleased, happy
aider	to help		

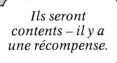

Talking about the future

Here are eight sentences in English for you to translate into French.

Her train will arrive at three.

They're going to go out this evening.

What are you going to do?

I'll go to Tourville tomorrow.

We'll know when they get here.

We'll look when we find the newspaper.

He'll see.

Will you come with me? (Use *vous* for "you".)

---

2 The French implies that the action is just going to happen, so in English you would often add "just".

Comparisons are when you say things like "taller" or "the tallest". In English you either make them like this (with "er" or "est"), or, for longer words, with "more" or "the most" (more important, the most important). Comparisons are made with either adjectives or adverbs (with most adverbs, you only use "more, the most"), for example, with an adjective, "She's taller/the tallest", or with an adverb, "It goes more/the most often".

Comparisons with adjectives

In French, to make comparisons with adjectives, you normally use the words *plus* (to mean "-er", "more") or *le/la/les plus* (to mean "the -est", "the most"). These go before the adjective and the adjective agrees with what it is describing. For example, with *chaud(e)* (warm), you say *l'eau plus chaude* (warmer water) or *l'eau la plus chaude* (the warmest water).

Remember: French adjectives come after the noun, but a few much used ones, such as *long(ue)*, come before,[1] for example, *le plus long chemin* (the longest path).

"Than" and "as … as"

In comparisons, to say "than" as in "He's taller than his sister", French uses *que*: *Il est plus grand que sa sœur*.
To say "(just) as … as", for example "(just) as tall as", you use *aussi … que*, so you say *aussi grand(e) que*. You can also use *aussi* on its own – *Son ami est aussi grand* (His friend's just as tall).

Comparisons with adverbs

Comparisons with adverbs are made as with adjectives, except there is no agreement – the adverb never changes. In addition, "est/the most" is always *le plus*. For example, with *lentement*, you say *Elle marche plus/le plus lentement* (She walks more/the most slowly).

Common exceptions

French has a few common words that do not use *plus* and *le plus* for comparisons. Here are the most useful (as the English translations show, they also have irregular comparisons in English):

Adjectives With *bon(ne)* (good), you say *meilleur(e), le/la/les meilleur(e)(s)* (better, the best).
With *mauvais(e)* (bad), you say *pire, le/la/les pire(s)* (worse, the worst).
Adverbs With *bien* (well), you say *mieux, le mieux* (better, the best).
With *mal* (badly), you say *pire, le pire* (worse, the worst).
With *peu* (few, little), you say *moins, le moins* (fewer/less, the fewest/least).

Speech bubble key

●*Est-ce que tu peux me prêter ta serviette?* Can you lend me your towel?
●*Pouah! Elle est aussi mouillée que la mienne.* Yuk! It's as wet as mine.
●*Salut Raoul! Est-ce que tu as ton bateau ici?* Hi Raoul! Have you got your boat here?
●*Oui, il est là-bas.* Yes, it's over there.

●*Est-ce qu'on peut l'emprunter? On veut aller à l'île des Pirates.* Can we borrow it? We want to go to Pirates' Island.
●*Oui, bien sûr. C'est le plus petit.* Yes, of course. It's the smallest.
●*Attention, une des rames est plus courte que l'autre …* Watch out, one

of the oars is shorter than the other …
●*Eh! On commence à tourner en rond.* Hey! We're starting to go around in circles.
●*Oui, Luc! Tu ne rames pas aussi vite que moi.* Yes, Luc! You're not rowing as fast as me.
●*Tu as la meilleure rame.* You've got

1 See list, page 50. **2** In comparisons you use the special set of pronouns, *moi, toi*, etc, for "I/me, you" etc. (see "A mixed set", page 28).

New words

la serviette	towel	*tourner en rond*	to go around in (a) circle(s)	*fort(e)*	strong
la rame	oar			*encore*	even, again, more
le cachot	dungeon	*ramer*	to row	*plein de*	lots of
le souterrain	underground passage, tunnel	*chaud(e)*	warm	*bizarre*	weird, strange, odd
la grille	gate	*mouillé(e)*	wet	*oh là!*	oh no!, oh dear!
		court(e)	short	*au bout de*	at/to the end of
prêter	to lend	*autre*	other, another		

Voilà le fort.

Il a plein de cachots et de souterrains

Il est encore plus vieux que la tour en ruine.

. . . mais on ne peut pas y descendre.

C'est bizarre, d'habitude la grille est fermée.

Oh, zut alors!

Eh, allez plus lentement.

Regardez, il y a quatre souterrains.

Oh là . . .

Venez ici! Regardez ça!

On ne peut plus sortir!

Quel est le plus long souterrain?

Marion, Luc and Céline know they must go to the end of the longest tunnel. But which one is it? Using footsteps as a measure (their feet are about the same size), Luc and Marion measure out a tunnel each and Céline does the other two. This is what they say when they compare measurements:

Mon souterrain n'est pas aussi long que le tien.

Mon premier souterrain était aussi long que le tien, mais mon deuxième est plus court.

Le mien est plus long que le premier de Céline.

Alors, quel est le plus long souterrain?

Can you answer Luc's question (in French)?

the best oar.
- *Mais non, je suis plus forte que toi!* No I haven't, I'm stronger than you!
- *Voilà le fort.* There's the fort.
- *Il est encore plus vieux que la tour en ruine.* It's even older than the ruined tower.
- *Il a plein de cachots et de souterrains* It's got lots of dungeons and tunnels
- *. . . mais on ne peut pas y descendre.* . . . but you can't go down there.
- *C'est bizarre, d'habitude la grille est fermée.* That's odd, normally the gate's shut.
- *Eh, allez plus lentement.* Hey, go more slowly.
- *Oh, zut alors!* Oh no!
- *Regardez, il y a quatre souterrains.* Look, there are four tunnels.
- *Oh là . . .* Oh no . . .
- *On ne peut plus sortir!* We can't get out now!
- *Venez ici! Regardez ça!* Come here! Look at this!

The conditional

In English, you make the conditional form of a verb with "would" (or just "'d"), for example "I would ask her, but she's too busy". To make the conditional of any French verb, you add the imperfect tense endings (see page 32) to the verb's future tense stem (see page 40). This means that the conditional of *marcher* looks as shown on the right.

Marcher ("would" form)

je marcherais	I would/'d walk
tu marcherais	you would walk
il/elle marcherait	he/she/it would walk
nous marcherions	we would walk
vous marcheriez	you would walk
ils/elles marcheraient	they would walk

Si (if)

The French for "if" is *si*. Like "if", it is used with different tenses depending on what you are saying. For anything that you are simply imagining, you use *si* with the imperfect and the conditional, for example *Si j'avais beaucoup d'argent, j'irais à New York* (If I had a lot of money, I'd go to New York). Otherwise, you use *si* with the present and future tenses, for example *Si j'ai assez d'argent, je viendrai avec toi* (If I have enough money, I'll come with you). *Si* shortens to *s'* in front of *il* or *ils*, for example *S'ils viennent avec nous, nous prendrons la voiture* (If they come with us, we'll take the car).

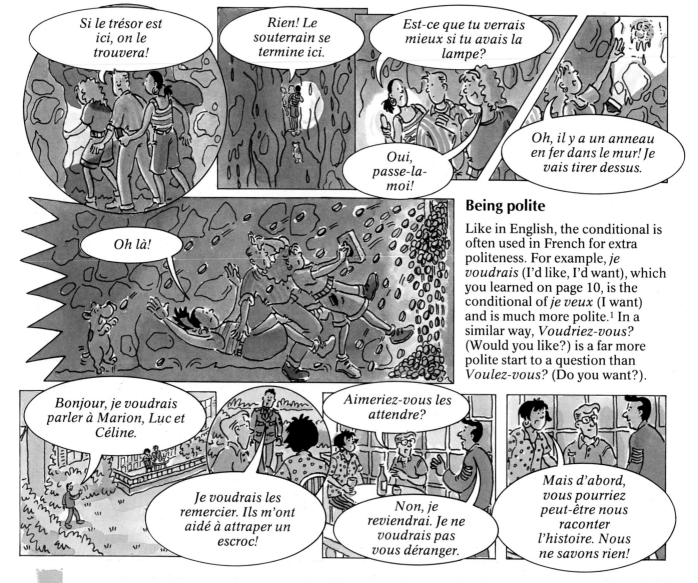

Being polite

Like in English, the conditional is often used in French for extra politeness. For example, *je voudrais* (I'd like, I'd want), which you learned on page 10, is the conditional of *je veux* (I want) and is much more polite.[1] In a similar way, *Voudriez-vous?* (Would you like?) is a far more polite start to a question than *Voulez-vous?* (Do you want?).

1 Notice how English often says "would like" rather than "would want".

New words

l'argent [m]	money	aider	to help
la voiture	car	déranger	to disturb
l'anneau(x) [m]	ring	retourner	to go back
le fer	iron	bouger	to move
l'histoire [f]	story, history	offrir*	to treat (someone to), to give, to offer
la marche	step		
la lumière	light		
l'entrée [f]	entrance	dépenser	to spend
la paire	pair	faire réparer	to have mended
le toit	roof		
la tante	aunt	si	if
le Canada	Canada	assez de/d'	enough
l'or [m]	gold	dessus	on top of (it), on (it)
		nouveau (nouvelle)²	new
se terminer	to end		
remercier	to thank	Maman	Mum

What if?

When the three get back to the maison Camembert, Marion asks her Mum what she would do if she suddenly had lots of money. To complete Aline's answers, you must put the verbs in brackets into the right form.

Maman, si tu avais beaucoup d'argent, qu'est-ce que tu ferais?

Je (dépenser) tout!

Je (faire) réparer le toit.

Tu (avoir) une nouvelle bicyclette.

Nous (aller) tous voir ma tante au Canada.

Eh bien, on a trouvé le trésor de Clément Camembert. Il y a plein d'or!

Bon ... On devrait chercher une sortie.

Regardez! De la lumière!

On en trouvera peut-être une si on retourne aux marches.

Ouf!

Céline, si tu bouges ces pierres, personne ne pourra voir l'entrée.

Je vais pouvoir offrir une nouvelle paire de rames à Raoul!

🗨 Speech bubble key

- *Si le trésor est ici, on le trouvera!* If the treasure's here, we'll find it!
- *Rien! Le souterrain se termine ici.* Nothing! The tunnel ends here.
- *Est-ce que tu verrais mieux si tu avais la lampe?* Would you see better if you had the torch?
- *Oui, passe-la-moi!* Yes, pass it to me!
- *Oh, il y a un anneau en fer dans le mur! Je vais tirer dessus.* Oh, there's an iron ring in the wall! I'm going to give it a pull.
- *Oh là!* Wow!
- *Bonjour, je voudrais parler à Marion, Luc et Céline.* Hello, I'd like to talk to Marion, Luc and Céline.
- *Je voudrais les remercier. Ils m'ont aidé à attraper un escroc!* I'd like to thank them. They helped me to catch a crook!
- *Aimeriez-vous les attendre?* Would you like to wait for them?
- *Non, je reviendrai. Je ne voudrais pas vous déranger.* No, I'll come back. I wouldn't want to disturb you.
- *Mais d'abord, vous pourriez peut-être nous raconter l'histoire. Nous ne savons rien!* But first, you could³ perhaps tell us the story. We don't know anything!
- *Bon ... On devrait chercher une sortie.* Right ... We should⁴ look for a way out.
- *On en trouvera peut-être une si on retourne aux marches.* We might find one if we go back to the steps.
- *Regardez! De la lumière!* Look! Light!
- *Ouf!* Phew!
- *Céline, si tu bouges ces pierres, personne ne pourra voir l'entrée.* Céline, if you move those rocks, nobody'll be able to see the entrance.
- *Je vais pouvoir offrir une nouvelle paire de rames à Raoul!* I'll be able to treat Raoul to a new pair of oars!

---

2 The masculine form is *nouvel* in front of a noun that begins with a vowel or "h".   3 Note: the conditional form of "can" is "could".   4 Note: the conditional form of "must, have to" is "should".

A letter to read

Here is a letter with a newspaper cutting that Marion sent to Luc and Céline after they went home to Paris. There is a lot of French for you to read through and make sense of. You can check how well you have done by looking at the English translations on page 57. There are also some useful words for writing a letter in French.

Letter-writing tips

If the date is Tuesday 7th September, you either write *mardi 7 septembre* (word for word, "Tuesday 7 September") or *le 7 septembre* ("the 7 September").[1] Days of the week and months are all listed on page 58.

For "Dear" at the start of a card or letter, you write *Cher* + a masculine name or *Chère* + a feminine one (*Chers* or *Chères* in the plural).

To sign off, you can write *Amitiés* (regards, best wishes) or either *Gros baisers* or *Grosses bises* (these mean "big kisses", but they are the equivalent of "love (from)" or "love and kisses").

---

lundi 2 septembre

Chers Luc et Céline,

Voici l'article de L'Écho de Tourville qui raconte notre histoire. Il est génial! Qu'allez-vous faire avec votre part de la récompense? Avec la mienne, je vais m'acheter une radiocassette.

Si votre mère est d'accord, je viendrai chez vous pendant les vacances de Noël, alors à bientôt, j'espère!

Grosses bises,

Marion

✝ L'ÉCHO DE TOURVILLE ✝
— Vendredi 30 août —

Le trésor de la famille Camembert

Marion Camembert avec ses amis Luc et Céline Meunier et son chien, Toudou.

Félix Filou, le voleur d'oiseaux rares qui voulait voler le trésor de la famille Camembert.

Pour Marion Camembert et ses amis Luc et Céline, cela a été un mois d'août passionnant. Ils ont trouvé un trésor et aidé la police à attraper un escroc, Félix Filou.

Il y a quelques mois, Filou était sur une des îles Wazorare. Il y cherchait des perroquets très rares qu'il voulait voler. Il est tombé sur une lettre de l'arrière-grand-père de Marion, Clément. C'était une vieille lettre adressée au grand-père de Marion, Joseph, et abandonnée sur l'île dans un vieux coffre après la mort de Clément. La lettre était le premier indice dans une chasse au trésor. Elle a mené Filou à Tourville où, bêtement, il l'a perdue. Luc et Céline, qui venaient passer quelques jours avec leur amie Marion, l'ont trouvée. Les trois adolescents ont réussi à trouver le trésor (de l'or), caché dans le vieux Fort des Pirates, avant l'escroc, et ils ont aidé la police à l'attraper.

Les trois héros ont aussi reçu une récompense de 15.000 francs de la police. Nous les félicitons!

New words

l'article [m]	article	*espérer*	to hope	*recevoir* (past participle: *reçu*)	to receive, to get
l'écho [m]	echo	*tomber sur*	to find by chance, to come across		
la part	part, share			*féliciter*	to congratulate
la radiocassette	radio cassette	*adresser*	to address		
le voleur	thief	*abandonner*	to abandon, to leave	*pendant*	during
le mois	month			*Noël*	Christmas
la mort	death	*mener*	to lead, to bring	*à bientôt*	see you soon
l'adolescent [m]	teenager	*perdre** (past participle: *perdu*)	to lose	*bêtement*	stupidly
le héros	hero	*passer*	to pass, to spend (time)		
être d'accord	to agree				

1 Note that in dates, you just use the number on its own. The only exception is the first of any month, for which you write *(le) 1er*. This stands for *(le) premier* ((the) first) – see page 58.

French grammar summary

This section brings together and summarizes the main areas of French grammar introduced in this book. It includes lists and tables that are useful for learning from. Remember that basic grammar terms, such as "noun" and "verb", are explained on page 5.

Nouns and *le, la, l'*

All French nouns have a gender. They are either masculine or feminine.

In the singular (when you are talking about one thing, e.g. "bridge" rather than the plural "bridges"), the word for "the" is *le* before masculine nouns and *la* before feminine nouns. However, if the noun begins with a vowel, the word for "the" is just *l'*, whatever the gender. *L'* is also used for many nouns that begin with "h".[1]

Examples:
le pont (the bridge)
la maison (the house)
l'aéroport [m] (the airport)
l'école [f] (the school)

Nouns and *un, une*

The word for "a" (or "an") is *un* before masculine nouns and *une* before feminine ones, for example:

un pont (a bridge)
une maison (a house)
un aéroport (an airport)
une école (a school)

Plural nouns

In the plural, most French nouns add an "s", for example:

deux ponts (two bridges)
trois maisons (three houses)

In English, "the" stays the same with plural nouns. French has a special, plural word for "the", *les*, which is used whatever the noun's gender, for example:

les ponts (the bridges)
les maisons (the houses)
les aéroports (the airports)
les écoles (the schools)

Unusual plurals

Some nouns do not follow the general rule about adding "s" in the plural. For some of these, there are rules you can follow, but for a few, you have to learn the plural form.

Nouns that end in "s", "x" or "z" stay the same in the plural, for example:

un mois, *deux mois* (a month, two months)
un nez, *deux nez* (a nose, two noses)
une voix, *deux voix* (a voice, two voices)

A few nouns add "x" in the plural. Nouns that end in "au", "eau" or "eu" add "x", and most nouns that end in "al" change their ending to "aux", for example:

le château, *les châteaux* (castle, castles)
le journal, *les journaux* (newspaper, newspapers)

A few nouns have a more complicated change in the plural, for example *l'œil* (eye) becomes *les yeux* (eyes).

"Some" and "any" (*du, de la, de l', des*)

In English, you use the same word for "some" with both singular and plural nouns, for instance "some coffee", "some chips". The French for "some" is *de* + the word for "the", so it changes depending on the word for "the" (*le, la, l'* or the plural *les*). Also, *de* and *le* contract to become *du*, and *de* and *les* contract to become *des*.

Examples:
le café (coffee) – *du café* (some coffee)
la glace (ice cream) – *de la glace* (some ice cream)
l'eau (water) – *de l'eau* (some water)
les frites (chips) – *des frites* (some chips)

In questions or in negative sentences (sentences with "not" or "n't"), the English word "some" changes to "any", for example, "Have you got any bread?", "I haven't seen any boys". In French questions, you use the same words for "any" as for "some" (*du, de la, de l', des*), but in negative sentences you always use *de* (or *d'* before a vowel and sometimes before an "h") without the word for "the", for example:

Je ne veux pas de café (I don't want any coffee)
Je ne veux pas de glace (I don't want any ice cream)
Je ne veux pas d'eau (I don't want any water)
Je ne veux pas de frites (I don't want any chips)

English can sometimes leave out the words "some" or "any", but you cannot do this in French. For example, you can say "I want some coffee" or just "I want coffee", but in French you have to say *Je veux du café*. Similarly, with questions or negative sentences, you can say "Do you want coffee?" and "I don't want coffee", but in French you must say *Veux-tu du café?* and *Je ne veux pas de café*.

Prepositions (*de* and *à*)

French prepositions (words like "of", "to", "at", "with", and so on) are easy to use. The most useful ones are listed on page 22. However, when using *de* (of, from) and *à* (at, to), you must remember the contractions which happen when they are used with *le* and *les*.

If *de* is used before *le* or *les*, the words contract in the same way as when *de* + "the" are used to mean "some" or "any" (see left), for example:

Elle sort du cinéma (She comes out of the cinema)
Elle sort de la tour (She comes out of the tower)
Elle sort de l'école (She comes out of the school)
Elle sort des toilettes (She comes out of the toilets)

À works in a similar way. It contracts with *le* to become *au* (at/to the) and with *les* to become *aux* (at/to the), for example:

Je vais au cinéma (I'm going to the cinema)
Je vais à la tour (I'm going to the tower)
Je vais à l'école (I'm going to the school)
Je vais aux toilettes (I'm going to the toilets)

French uses *de* and *à* for saying whose something is, as in "It's Marion's jumper" or "It's the girl's". This is explained on page 12.

1 When learning nouns that begin with "h", learn them with the word for "the", for example *l'homme* [m] (man), *l'habitude* [f] (habit), *le haut* (top), *la haie* (hedge), so that you know whether to use *le, la* or *l'*. The nouns that are used with *l'* are also used with the short versions of words like *de* or *que*, that is, *d', qu'* and so on. Notice that in word lists, nouns are usually listed with *le* or *la*, or with *l'* and a bracketed "m" for "masculine" or "f" for "feminine", so that you know their gender.

Adjectives

In French, most adjectives come after the noun they are used with, for example:

noir (black) – *un chat noir* (a black cat)
blanc (white) – *un chat blanc* (a white cat)

However, a few common adjectives such as *gros* (big, fat) are normally put in front of the noun, for example *Un gros chat* (A big cat) – see the list in the box to the right.

To make comparisons using adjectives – to say, for example, "He is as tall as my sister" or "She is more important than Rob", you use *aussi . . . que* (as . . . as) and *plus . . . que* (more . . . than). For a detailed explanation of comparisons, see page 44.

Agreement of adjectives

French adjectives agree with the noun (or pronoun) they are used with. This means that they have slightly different forms for the two genders and for the plurals. Usually, the basic adjective (which is the masculine singular form) adds "e" in the feminine, "s" in the plural if the noun is masculine, and "es" in the plural if the noun is feminine. For example, with *noir* (black), you say:

le chat noir (the black cat)
la souris noire (the black mouse)
les chats noirs (the black cats)
les souris noires (the black mice)

If you have a plural that is a mixture of masculine and feminine, you use the masculine plural, for example:

les chats et les souris noirs (the black cats and mice).

As you can see from the list of adjectives above right, some adjectives do not simply add "e" in the feminine. They may add another letter, or change entirely. For example, the feminine of *gros* is *grosse* and the feminine of *beau* is *belle*. Adjectives that already end in "e" stay the same in the feminine, and a few adjectives never change at all, for example *marron* (brown).

Adjectives that come before the noun

beau/bel (belle)	beautiful, handsome, fine
bon(ne)	good
gentil(le)	nice, kind
grand(e)	big, tall
gros(se)	big, fat
haut(e)	high
jeune	young
joli(e)	pretty
long(ue)	long
mauvais(e)	bad
petit(e)	small, little
vieux/vieil (vieille)	old

Two adjectives shown here have two different masculine forms (*beau/bel, vieux/vieil*). A few adjectives are like this. The second, extra masculine form is used in front of masculine nouns beginning with a vowel and masculine nouns beginning with "h" that use *l'* for "the".

Word lists always show the feminine forms of adjectives as in the box above (that is, with the extra letters needed to form the feminine shown in brackets), e.g. *noir(e)* means the masculine is *noir* and the feminine is *noire, gros(se)* means the two forms are *gros* [m] and *grosse* [f]). When the feminine form is very different, it is given in full, for example *beau/bel (belle)*.

"My", "your", "his", "her", etc.

These words are a kind of adjective. In French, the words for "my", "your", and so on, agree with the noun they are used with. This table shows you which word to use:

	with a masculine noun	with a feminine noun	with a plural noun
my	*mon*	*ma*	*mes*
your	*ton*	*ta*	*tes*
his/her/its	*son*	*sa*	*ses*
our	*notre*	*notre*	*nos*
your	*votre*	*votre*	*vos*
their	*leur*	*leur*	*leurs*

For example, with *le sac*, you would say *son sac* (his/her bag), with *la valise*, you would say *sa valise* (his/her suitcase), and in the plural, *ses sacs* (his/her bags) or *ses valises* (his/her suitcases).

However, if a feminine noun begins with a vowel or "h", you use the masculine *mon, ton* and *son*, for example *mon école* (my school).

As you can see, there are two sets of words for "your". You use *ton, ta* or *tes* where you would use *tu* for "you", and *votre* or *vos* where you would use *vous*. The section below explains the difference between *tu* (you) and *vous* (you).

"I", "you", "he", "she", etc. (*je, tu, il, elle*, etc.)

The French for "I" is *je*. It shortens to *j'* in front of a vowel or "h", for example, you say *je suis* (I am), but *j'aime* (I like) and *j'habite* (I live).

The French for "you" is either *tu* or *vous*. You say *tu* to a friend or a relative – it is called the familiar form.

Vous is the polite form, and it is also the plural form. This means that you use it when talking to someone you do not know well or someone older than you, and you also use it when talking to more than one person (even when you know them well).

Whenever you are not sure whether you should say *tu* or *vous* to someone, say *vous*. If the person wants you to say *tu*, they will let you know. (There is a special verb, *tutoyer*, which means "to say *tu*". Listen out for *Tu peux me tutoyer*. It means "You can say *tu* to me".) Usually, though, when a child or teenager talks to another child or teenager, *tu* is used, even at a first encounter.

The French for "he" is *il*, and the French for "she" is *elle*. To say "it", you use *il* or *elle* depending on the gender of the noun or pronoun you are referring to. You use *il* for anything masculine and *elle* for anything feminine. For example, if talking about *le sac* (bag), you say *Il est là* (It is there), but for *la valise* (suitcase), you say *Elle est là* (It is there).

The French for "we" is *nous*.

The French for "they" is *ils* in the masculine and *elles* in the feminine. This means that if "they" refers to some boys or men, or to some masculine things (for example *des sacs*), you say *ils*. If "they" refers to some girls or women, or to some feminine things (for example *des valises*), you say *elles*. For a mixture of masculine and feminine, the masculine *ils* is used.

Verbs

Most French verbs fall into one of two main groups. The most important one is the "er" group. Verbs in this group all end in "er" in the infinitive (basic) form, for example *marcher* (to walk – see below).[1]

The other group which quite a few verbs fall into is the "ir" group. Most verbs in this group follow the pattern shown by *choisir* (to choose – see right). A few "ir" verbs follow a slightly different "ir" pattern, shown by *partir* (to go (away), to leave – see right).

Verbs that do not fall into a group are called irregular, for example *avoir* (to have (got)), *être* (to be) and *faire* (to do). You have to learn them, and their various forms, individually. Many of the most useful irregular verbs are shown on pages 54-55.

The present tense – "er" and "ir" verbs

Verbs change to show when their action takes place. Tenses are the different forms that verbs adopt to do this. For example, "I/you/we/they have" and "he/she/it has" are the present tense forms of "to have"; the past tense is "had".

To make the present tense of "er" verbs, you take the verb's stem (the infinitive form, for instance *marcher*, minus "er") and you add the present tense endings shown below by the present tense of *marcher*. For "ir" verbs, the stem is the infinitive verb minus "ir", and you add the endings shown by the present of *choisir* – or, for a few verbs, the present of *partir*.

Marcher (to walk) – present tense

je marche	I walk (am walking)
tu marches	you walk
il/elle marche	he/she/it walks
nous marchons	we walk
vous marchez	you walk
ils/elles marchent	they walk

Choisir (to choose) – present tense

je choisis	I choose (am choosing)
tu choisis	you choose
il/elle choisit	he/she/it chooses
nous choisissons	we choose
vous choisissez	you choose
ils/elles choisissent	they choose

Partir (to go (away), to leave) – present tense

je pars	I leave (am leaving)
tu pars	you leave
il/elle part	he/she/it leaves
nous partons	we leave
vous partez	you leave
ils/elles partent	they leave

"Ir" verbs that follow the pattern of *partir* instead of *choisir* include *dormir* (to sleep), *mentir* (to lie), *sentir* (to feel, to smell), *servir* (to serve) and *sortir* (to go out), for example *Tu mens* (You're lying).

As you can see, the French present tense is used for an action that is happening now or one that happens regularly. This means that *je marche* can either mean "I walk" or "I am/I'm walking". As in English, the present is also sometimes used instead of the future tense for something that is going to happen. For example, *J'arrive le 3 août* means literally "I arrive on the 3rd of August" but can be translated as "I'll arrive on the 3rd of August" or "I'll be arriving on the 3rd of August".

Personal pronouns

Je (I), *tu* (you), *il* (he, it), *elle* (she, it), *nous* (we), *vous* (you), *ils* and *elles* (they) (see page 50) are called personal pronouns. This is because they stand in for the name of a person or thing.

These pronouns sometimes change when they are the object of a verb (rather than its subject), for example in English, "I" becomes "me" ("I like dogs" but "Rover likes me").

With some of its personal pronouns, French also makes this distinction, but in addition, it sometimes makes a difference between the two kinds of object. In "Rover likes her", "her" is a direct object, but in "Rover gives her the bone" (or "Rover gives the bone to her"), "her" is an indirect object. Some French personal pronouns have a different form for the direct object and the indirect object. This table shows you all the forms:

subject	direct object
je/j' (I)	*me/m'* (me)
tu (you)	*te/t'* (you)
il (he/it)	*le/l'* (him/it)
elle (she/it)	*la/l'* (her/it)
nous (we)	*nous* (us)
vous (you)	*vous* (you)
ils (they)	*les* (them)
elles (they)	*les* (them)

indirect object
me/m' ((to) me)
te/t' ((to) you)
lui ((to) him/it)
lui ((to) her/it)
nous ((to) us)
vous ((to) you)
leur ((to) them)
leur ((to) them

In French, the indirect object pronoun already means "to me/you/him", etc, so you do not translate "to" into French as a separate word. In the table, "to" is bracketed because it is not always needed in English – you can say "He passes the book to me" or "He passes me the book".

Object pronouns and word order

French personal pronouns normally go before the verb (*Rover me donne l'os* – Rover gives me the bone).[2] If a sentence has more than one object pronoun, the pronouns are always used in a set order. This table summarizes the order:

1	2	3
me	*le/l'*	*lui*
te	*la/l'*	*leur*
nous	*les*	
vous		

For example, because *vous* must come before *la*, you would say, talking about *une glace* (an ice cream), *Je vous la passe* (I'm passing it to you) or, because *le* must come before *leur*, talking about *un livre* (a book), you would say *Il le leur donne* (He's giving it to them).

---

1 *Aller* (to go) looks like an "er" verb, but it is an irregular verb (see page 54). **2** The exception is when the verb is in the imperative (see page 53).

Moi, toi, lui, etc. (me, you, him, etc.)

In a few cases, French does not use the same personal pronouns as those set out in the three tables on page 51. It has another, mixed set of pronouns, *moi* (I, me), *toi* (you – familiar form), *lui* (he, him, it), *elle (she, her, it), nous (we, us), vous* (you – polite and plural form), *eux* (they, them – masculine), *elles* (they, them – feminine).

You use this set of pronouns

1) after prepositions (words like "of", "to", "at", etc.), for example *Ton pull est derrière toi* (Your jumper's behind you);

2) after *c'est*, for example *C'est lui* (It's him);

3) in short answers and exclamations, for example *Qui est là? Moi!* (Who's there? Me!);

4) in comparisons, after *que* (than) and *aussi . . . que* (as . . . as), for example *plus grand que moi* (taller than me), *aussi grand que toi* (as tall as you).

With imperative verbs (see page 53), you use *moi* and *toi* instead of the standard object pronouns *me* and *te*, but otherwise you use the standard ones.

Verbs – the imperfect tense

In French, you use the imperfect tense for talking about events that were in the process of happening at a particular point in the past – where English uses "was/were + (verb + ing)", as in "I was cycling" or "we were watching TV".

French also uses the imperfect for an event that happened often or regularly – where English can say "I often cycled", "I cycled to school each day" or "I used to cycle to school".

To form the imperfect tense, you take the present tense *nous* form, drop the *-ons* ending, and add one of a set of imperfect endings. These endings are *-ais, -ais, -ions, -iez* and *-aient*. The imperfect of *marcher* is shown above right. All French verbs except *être* form the imperfect like this. (The imperfect of *être* is shown on page 55.)

Marcher (imperfect tense)

je marchais	I was walking/walked (often)
tu marchais	you were walking
il/elle marchait	he/she/it was walking
nous marchions	we were walking
vous marchiez	you were walking
ils/elles marchaient	they were walking

The perfect tense

French uses the perfect tense[1] to talk about once-only past events – events that happened once at the time you are talking about or in the story you are telling. For example, in English, "That morning he cycled to school. He skidded on a banana skin and ended up in the pond".

French also uses the perfect tense where, for example, English uses have/has, as in "She has travelled a lot" or "I have read two of her books".

The French perfect tense is made of two bits. For most verbs, it is made from the present tense of *avoir* (to have)[2] and a special form of the verb you are using, called the past participle. For example, the past participle of *marcher* is *marché*, so the perfect tense *je* form of *marcher* is *j'ai marché* (I have walked, I walked).

For a few verbs, the perfect is made from the present tense of *être*[2] (see below) and the past participle, for example, the perfect tense *je* form of *monter* is *je suis monté* (I have been upstairs, I went upstairs).

The past participle

To form the past participle of "er" verbs, you just add "é" to the stem (the infinitive minus the "er" ending), for example *marché*. For "ir" verbs, you just add "i" to the stem (the infinitive minus "ir"), for example *choisi*.

For irregular verbs (verbs which do not follow the "er" or "ir" patterns), you have to learn the past participle.

"Être verbs"

Just like the verbs that form the perfect tense with *avoir*, some verbs that use *être* are regular, and others are irregular. Most of them involve either a change of place (for example *entrer* – to go in, to enter) or of state (for example *devenir* – to become). This is a useful thing to remember. This list shows most of the regular "*être* verbs":

arriver	to arrive, to get somewhere
entrer	to go in, to enter
monter	to go up(stairs)
partir	to leave, to go off
rentrer	to go home
rester	to stay
retourner	to go back, to return
sortir	to go out
tomber	to fall (over)

All reflexive verbs (see page 53) also form the perfect tense with *être*.

Past participles of irregular verbs

Here are two lists of useful irregular verbs with their past participle forms which you should try to learn. The first list shows irregular verbs that form the perfect with *avoir*. The second one shows irregular verbs that form the perfect with *être*.

Irregular "avoir verbs"

avoir (past participle: *eu*)	to have (got)
attendre (attendu)	to wait
connaître (connu)	to know
devoir (dû)	to have to
entendre (entendu)	to hear
être (été)	to be
faire (fait)	to do
mettre (mis)	to put
ouvrir (ouvert)	to open
perdre (perdu)	to lose
prendre (pris)	to take
pouvoir (pu)	to be able
recevoir (reçu)	to receive, to get
savoir (su)	to know
tenir (tenu)	to hold
voir (vu)	to see
vouloir (voulu)	to want

Irregular "être verbs"

aller (allé)	to go
descendre (descendu)	to go down(stairs)
devenir (devenu)	to become
mourir (mort)	to die
naître (né)	to be born
revenir (revenu)	to come back
venir (venu)	to come

1 Note that the full name of the perfect tense is the "present perfect tense". **2** Bear in mind that *avoir* and *être* are irregular – you can find their present tenses on pages 54-55.

Agreement of the past participle in the perfect tense

For *avoir* verbs, the past participle normally does not change or agree with anything. However, if there is a direct object before the verb, the past participle agrees with it like an adjective. For example, when talking about a feminine thing such as *une montre* (a watch), to say "I've taken it", you do not say *Je l'ai pris* but *Je l'ai prise*.

It is important to get the agreement right as it can alter the sound: *pris* is said "pree", but *prise* (or the feminine plural *prises*) is said "preez".

For *être* verbs, the past participle always agrees with the subject, for example *Il est sorti* (He went out), *Elle est sortie* (She went out), *Ils sont sortis* (They [m] went out) and *Elles sont sorties* (They [f] went out). Remember that reflexive verbs also form the perfect tense with *être*, and this rule on agreement also usually applies to them (see top right).

The future tense

The French future tense is usually used where English uses its future tense – where, for example, English says "I will (or "I'll") write the letter tomorrow".

To form the future tense of most French verbs, you take the infinitive form and add the following endings: *-ai, -as, -a, -ons, -ez, -ont*. For example, see the future tense of *marcher* below.

Marcher (future tense)

je marcherai	I will walk
tu marcheras	you will walk
il/elle marchera	he/she/it will walk
nous marcherons	we will walk
vous marcherez	you will walk
ils/elles marcheront	they will walk

For a few verbs, forming the future tense is a bit more complicated. Verbs with an infinitive that ends in "re" lose the "e" and then add the future tense endings, so for *prendre* (to take), you say *je prendrai* (I will take).

There are also a small number of verbs which have a special future tense stem (to which you add the future endings), for example, for *aller* (to go) the stem is *ir-*, so the *je* form is *j'irai*, the *tu* form, *tu iras*, and so on. Many of the most useful of these future stems are shown on page 40, and the list of irregular verbs with their various forms on pages 54-55 also shows irregular future tenses.

The imperative

The imperative form of a verb is used when you want to give a command – where, in English, for example, you say "Come here!".

To make the imperative, you take the verb's present tense *tu* or *vous* forms and you leave out the words *tu* and *vous*, for example *Choisis!* or *Choisissez!* (Choose!). With "er" verbs, however, you also drop the "s" on the end of the *tu* form, for example *Marche!* or *Marchez!* (Walk!).

The imperative form of irregular verbs is shown on pages 54-55, and some useful, much used imperatives are shown on page 14.

When you use an imperative verb with an object pronoun, this goes after the verb, with a hyphen in between. If there are two pronouns, they both go after the verb (the direct object goes first) and there are two hyphens, for example:

Cherche-la (Look for her)
Donne-le-moi (Give it to me)

The conditional

For all French verbs, the conditional form (the "would" form, as in "I would buy it now, but I haven't got any money") is made by taking the verb's future tense stem (for most verbs, this is the infinitive form – see left) and adding the following endings: *-ais, -ais, -ait, -ions, -iez, -aient* (these are the same as the imperfect tense endings). As an example, here is the conditional of *marcher*:

je marcherais	I would/'d walk
tu marcherais	you would walk
il/elle marcherait	he/she/it would walk
nous marcherions	we would walk
vous marcheriez	you would walk
ils/elles marcheraient	they would walk

Reflexive verbs

Reflexive verbs are verbs such as *se lever* (to get up) that always begin with the words *me* (myself), *te* (yourself), *se* (him-/her-/itself, oneself), *nous* (ourselves), *vous* (yourself/selves), *se* (plural: themselves). Their infinitive form always begins with the word *se* (see the present tense of *se lever*, below). *Me, te* and *se* become *m', t', s'* if the actual verb begins with a vowel or "h", for example *s'habiller*.

Reflexive verbs can be regular or irregular. Reflexive "er" and "ir" verbs follow the "er" and "ir" patterns, and irregular reflexive verbs have to be learnt just like other irregular verbs.

Se lever (to get up) – present tense

je me lève	I get up
tu te lèves	you get up
il/elle se lève	he/she/it gets up
nous nous levons	we get up
vous vous levez	they get up
ils/elles se lèvent	they get up

All reflexive verbs form the perfect tense with *être*, for example:

Je me suis levé(e) (I got up, I have got up)

In the perfect, the verb always agrees with the subject (so if *je* refers to a girl, you say *je me suis levée*). A few reflexive verbs can be used with a direct object, though, and in those instances, there is no agreement, for example:

Je me suis lavé les mains (I washed my hands)

In the imperative, the small reflexive words are kept, but they go after the verb plus a hyphen, and *te* changes to *toi*, for example:

Lève-toi (Get up)
Levez-vous (Get up)

Negatives

Negative sentences are sentences with "not" (or "n't") in them, for example "I am not tired" or "I have not (or "haven't") got the time". In English you also often have to use "do" or "can" to make a negative sentence (you say "I don't smoke" and "I can't see", not "I smoke not" and "I see not"). In French, the verb does not change like this.

The French for not is *ne . . . pas* (*ne* shortens to *n'* in front of a vowel or "h"). The words go on either side of the verb, for example *je suis* (I am) becomes *je ne suis pas* (I am not) and *j'arrive* (I'm arriving) becomes *je n'arrive pas* (I'm not arriving).

With a perfect tense verb, *ne . . . pas* goes around the first bit of the verb (the *être* or *avoir* bit), for example *j'ai trouvé* (I have found) becomes *je n'ai pas trouvé* (I haven't found).

Remember that in negative sentences, *du*, *de la*, *de l'* and *des* are all replaced by *de*, for example *Je veux du café* (I want some coffee) becomes *Je ne veux pas de café* (I don't want any coffee).

Making questions

French has two methods for making questions.

Method 1 You put *est-ce que* at the start of a sentence, for example *Est-ce que tu veux du café?* (Do you want any coffee?).

Method 2 You put the subject after the verb, with a hyphen in between, for example *Veux-tu du café?* (Do you want any coffee?).

Both methods are easy to use if the subject is *tu*, *il(s)*, *elle(s)*, *nous* or *vous*, but you should avoid method 2 if the subject is *je* or a name or noun. a) and b) below explain why.

a) With *je*, French people avoid method 2 because it can sound pompous. Some verbs also change a bit before *je*, for instance *je peux* becomes *puis-je*, and these special *je* forms sound old-fashioned.

b) With a name or noun, method 2 needs to be adapted, and it can get more complicated, for example, you say *Céline veut-elle du café?* (Does Céline want any coffee?) or *Ton chien veut-il de l'eau?* (Does your dog want water?). As you can see, the name or noun goes first, followed by the verb, a hyphen and a personal pronoun.

When using method 2, if ever the verb ends in a vowel and the subject is *il(s)* or *elle(s)*, you insert "-t-" in between, for example *A-t-elle du café?* (Has she got coffee?). In spoken French, this "t" is sounded.

With question words such as *où?* (where? – see list of question words on page 16), put the question word at the start of the question. Then, if the subject is *tu*, *il(s)*, *elle(s)*, *nous* or *vous*, you can use either method, for example:

Où est-ce que tu vas? (Where are you going?)
Où vas-tu? (Where are you going?)

With a question word and *je* as the subject, use method 1 (or you will have the same problems as outlined earlier), for example:

Où est-ce que je peux manger? (Where can I eat?)

With a question word and a name or noun as the subject, use method 1 for long questions (anything longer than question word + verb + subject) and method 2 for short questions (but without a hyphen), for example:

Où est-ce que Céline fait ses courses? (Where does Céline do her shopping?)
Où va Céline? (Where is Céline going?)

In all questions made according to method 2, if the verb is in the perfect tense, the subject goes after the first bit of the verb, for example:

tu es allé (you went) – *Où es-tu allé?* (Where did you go?)
vous avez mangé (you ate) – *Où avez-vous mangé?* (Where did you eat?)

Irregular verbs

Many of the most commonly used verbs in French are irregular. *Être* (to be) and *avoir* (to have) are especially important because they are used to form other tenses, in particular the perfect tense.

Some of the most useful irregular verbs are shown here in the tenses and forms you will need. For each verb, the present tense and the future tense *je* form are given, as well as the past participle and imperative forms.

Remember:
1) to make the imperfect tense, take the present tense *nous* form, drop *-ons* and add *-ais*, *-ais*, *-ait*, *-ions*, *-iez* or *-aient*. *Être* is an exception so its imperfect is shown;

2) for the perfect tense, use the present tense of *avoir* or *être* + the verb's past participle;

3) for the future tense, take the future stem – shown by the *je* form (minus *-ai*), and add *-ai*, *-as*, *-a*, *-ons*, *-ez*, *-ont*;

4) for the conditional form, take the future stem and add *-ais*, *-ais*, *-ait*, *-ions*, *-iez* or *-aient*.

Aller (to go)

present tense

je vais	I go (am going)
tu vas	you go
il/elle va	he/she/it goes
nous allons	we go
vous allez	you go
ils/elles vont	they go

future tense
j'irai (I will/I'll go)

past participle
allé (been)

imperative
va, allez (go)

Avoir (to have (got))

present tense

j'ai	I have (got) (am having)
tu as	you have (got)
il/elle a	he/she/it has (got)
nous avons	we have (got)
vous avez	you have (got)
ils/elles ont	they have (got)

future tense
j'aurai (I will/I'll have (got))

past participle
eu (had, got, gotten)

imperative
aie, ayez (have)

Connaître (to know)

present tense

je connais	I know
tu connais	you know
il/elle connaît	he/she/it knows
nous connaissons	we know
vous connaissez	you know
ils/elles connaissent	they know

future tense
je connaîtrai (I will/I'll know)

past participle
connu (known)

imperative
connais, connaissez (know)

Devoir (to have to, must)

present tense

je dois	I must
tu dois	you must
il/elle doit	he/she/it must
nous devons	we must
vous devez	you must
ils/elles doivent	they must

future tense
je devrai (I will/I'll have to)

past participle
dû (no accent in the feminine or plural: *due, du(e)s* (had to)

imperative
not used

Être (to be)

present tense

je suis	I am/I'm (am being)
tu es	you are
il/elle est	he/she/it is
nous sommes	we are
vous êtes	you are
ils/elles sont	they are

imperfect tense

j'étais	I was
tu étais	you were
il/elle était	he/she/it was
nous étions	we were
vous étiez	you were
ils/elles étaient	they were

future tense
je serai (I will/I'll be)

past participle
été (been)

imperative
sois, soyez (be)

Faire (to do)

present tense

je fais	I do (am doing)
tu fais	you do
il/elle fait	he/she/it does
nous faisons	we do
vous faites	you do
ils/elles font	they do

future tense
je ferai (I will/I'll do)

past participle
fait (done)

imperative
fais, faites (do)

Pouvoir (to be able to, can)

present tense

je peux	I can
tu peux	you can
il/elle peut	he/she/it can
nous pouvons	we can
vous pouvez	you can
ils/elles peuvent	they can

future tense
je pourrai (I will/I'll be able to)

past participle
pu (been able to)

imperative
not used

Prendre (to take)

present tense

je prends	I take (am taking)
tu prends	you take
il/elle prend	he/she/it takes
nous prenons	we take
vous prenez	you take
ils/elles prennent	they take

future tense
je prendrai (I will/I'll take)

past participle
pris (taken)

imperative
prends, prenez (take)

Savoir (to know)

present tense

je sais	I know
tu sais	you know
il/elle sait	he/she/it knows
nous savons	we know
vous savez	you know
ils/elles savent	they know

future tense
je saurai (I will/I'll know)

past participle
su (known)

imperative
sache, sachez (know)

Tenir (to hold)

present tense

je tiens	I hold (am holding)
tu tiens	you hold
il/elle tient	he/she/it holds
nous tenons	we hold
vous tenez	you hold
ils/elles tiennent	they hold

future tense
je tiendrai (I will/I'll hold)

past participle
tenu (held)

imperative
tiens, tenez (hold)

Venir (to come)

present tense

je viens	I come (am coming)
tu viens	you come
il/elle vient	he/she/it comes
nous venons	we come
vous venez	you come
ils/elles viennent	they come

future tense
je viendrai (I will/I'll come)

past participle
venu (come)

imperative
viens, venez (come)

Vouloir (to want (to))

present tense

je veux	I want (am wanting)
tu veux	you want
il/elle veut	he/she/it wants
nous voulons	we want
vous voulez	you want
ils/elles veulent	they want

future tense
je voudrai (I will/I'll want)

past participle
voulu (wanted)

imperative
veuille, veuillez (want)[1]

1 *Veuillez* is often used with an infinitive verb to ask someone very politely to do something, e.g. *Veuillez me suivre* (Please follow me).

Answers to quizzes and puzzles

Page 7 Getting to the Camembert house

un café
un village
un lac
une ferme
un pont

Page 9 What is their luggage like?

2 *Ses valises sont grises.*
3 *Son sac est bleu.*
4 *Sa valise est verte.*
5 *Sa serviette est rouge.*
6 *Son sac à dos est jaune.*

Page 11 The mysterious letter

Une île déserte, 1893

Mon cher fils Joseph,

   *Je suis un vieil homme. Je suis **seul** sur mon île **déserte** et **ma** maison près de Tourville est vide. J'ai un secret. Je suis très **riche**. Maintenant mon trésor est **ton** trésor. Ma maison **cache** le premier indice. D'abord tu **cherches** les deux **bateaux**.*

Adieu, Clément Camembert

A desert island, 1893

My dear son Joseph,

   I am an old man. I am alone on my desert island, and my house near Tourville is empty. I have a secret. I am very wealthy. Now my treasure is your treasure. My house hides the first clue. First of all you're looking for the two ships.

Farewell, Clément Camembert

Page 13 *À qui est . . . ?*

2 *Cette table est aux voisins.*
3 *Cette veste est au locataire.*
4 *Cette chemise est à Aline.*
5 *Ce jean est à Luc.*
6 *Ces outils sont au maçon.*

Page 15 The way to the old church

Tournez à gauche.
Traversez le pont.
Prenez le deuxième chemin à gauche.
Tournez à droite.

Page 17 Shopping quiz

Où est le supermarché?
Je voudrais une glace. Combien coûtent-elles? OR . . . Combien est-ce qu'elles coûtent?
Quels parfums avez-vous? OR Quels parfums est-ce que vous avez?
Est-ce que je peux avoir un kilo de pommes, s'il vous plaît?
Pouvez-vous porter mon panier? OR Est-ce que vous pouvez porter mon panier?

What does the letter mean?

Clément Camembert est l'arrière-grand-père de Marion.
Les deux bateaux sont des tableaux.
Ils doivent visiter l'atelier (d'Aline/de la mère de Marion).

Page 19 The first clue

Il n'y a pas de dés.
Il n'y a pas de bougie.
Il n'y a pas d'oiseau.
Il n'y a pas de livre.
Il n'y a pas de chapeau haut de forme.

Page 21 Crossword puzzle

Across
 1 *il prend*
 5 *clés*
 6 *du thé*
 7 *sent*
 8 *part*
10 *ta*
11 *tu mens*

Down
 2 *partons*
 3 *de la glace*
 4 *des frites*
 7 *sort*
 9 *du*

Page 23 The clue from the inn

(Elle/la vache est) sur la colline.
(Il/le chien est) sous l'arbre (OR à côté de l'arbre OR près de l'arbre).
(Il/le banc est) en face de la fontaine (OR devant/à côté de/près de la fontaine).
(Elle/la ferme) est à côté de l'église (OR près de l'église).

Céline's sentence ends:

. . . à l'école.

Page 25 A postcard from Céline

Les voisins (des parents de Marion) ont une chèvre.
Céline et Luc/Ils dorment dans les tentes (qui sont dans le jardin).
Ils mangent et se lavent dans la maison.
Céline/Elle se réveille à six heures (du matin).
Luc/Il se réveille à huit heures (du matin).
Céline et Luc/Ils se couchent à neuf heures et demie ou dix heures (du soir).

Page 27 Mix and match

Nous ne pouvons pas venir maintenant parce que nous sommes en train de manger.
Je prends ta bicyclette pour aller à Port-le-Vieux.
Nous connaissons Madame Cachet parce qu'elle travaille à la pharmacie.
Tais-toi! Je dois réfléchir parce que c'est très difficile.
Elle va à Tourville pour faire des courses.
Le mécanicien est ici parce que la machine est cassée.

Page 29 The postcard jigsaw

Monsieur Félix Filou
3, rue de la Gare
Paris 75018

Cher Félix,

Merci pour ta lettre. Oui, Jules et Emma Champlein habitent près de Tourville. Tu me demandes leur adresse. La voici: la Ferme des Trois Chênes, Route du Pont Neuf, près de Port-le-Vieux. Mais pourquoi Tourville? Ce n'est pas une ville bien passionnante. Enfin, ils ont probablement une chambre pour toi et je te les recommande. On mange bien chez eux et c'est tranquille. Alors, bonnes vacances!

Nadine

Mr Félix Filou
3 rue de la Gare
Paris 75018

Dear Félix,

Thank you for your letter. Yes, Jules and Emma Champlein live near Tourville. You ask me for their address. Here it is: the Trois Chênes farm, Route du Pont Neuf, near Port-le-Vieux. But why Tourville? It's not a very exciting town. Anyhow, they probably have a room for you and I recommend them to you. You eat well at their place and it's quiet. So, have a good holiday!

Nadine

Page 31   Picture puzzle

1c   2d   3b   4f   5e   6a

Page 33   Clément Camembert's disappearance

Wazorareville

Sir,
Sadly, your father is very probably dead. He knew our islands well, but at the time of his disappearance, he was looking for plants on some dangerous and very remote islands. He was with two botanist friends. They had a good boat, but it was the stormy season.

Pedro Paté, Governor of the islands

Page 35   Telling a story

Deux copains, Fred et Loïc, faisaient des courses. Ils cherchaient des jeans. Dans un magasin, ils ont trouvé des clés dans la poche d'un jean. Ils les ont données au propriétaire. "Les clés de mon coffre-fort! Merci! Je les ai perdues hier. Je les ai cherchées partout, mais je ne les ai pas trouvées." Comme récompense, il leur a donné des jeans.

Page 37   Say it in French

*Monsieur Filou a cherché la tour en ruine, mais il ne l'a pas trouvée.
Céline, Luc et Marion sont allés à la ferme.
Ils ont trouvé Monsieur Filou.
Il ne les a pas vus.
Céline et Marion se sont cachées sous la fenêtre.*

Page 39   The writing on the tower

We have kept this ruined tower because it is a sacred monument for the inhabitants of Tourville.
The pirates of Pirate Island destroyed it three years ago, but now, we have got our revenge. We have won our last battle against them, we have expelled them from their fort on the island and they have disappeared from our country.

Page 41   The false trail

Mon fils, Maintenant tu as trouvé tous les indices que j'ai laissés. Voici ta dernière tâche. Elle sera difficile. Il faudra aller à la gendarmerie de Port-le-Vieux. Tu verras une fenêtre sans barreaux. Tu entreras par là. À l'intérieur, tu trouveras un mur avec des panneaux en bois. Tous mes bijoux et ma fortune seront là. Adieu. C.C.

My son, Now you have found all the clues I left. Here is your last task. It will be difficult. You will have to go to the police station in Port-le-Vieux. You will see one window without bars. You will go in that way. Inside you will find one wall with wooden panels. All my jewels and my fortune will be there. Farewell. C.C.

Page 43   Talking about the future

*Son train arrivera à trois heures.
Ils/Elles vont sortir ce soir.
Qu'est-ce que tu vas faire? OR Que vas-tu faire? OR Qu'est-ce que vous allez faire? OR Qu'allez-vous faire?
J'irai à Tourville demain.
Nous saurons/On saura quand ils arriveront.
Nous regarderons quand nous trouverons le journal OR On regardera quand on trouvera le journal.
Il verra.
Est-ce que vous viendrez avec moi?/ Viendrez-vous avec moi?*

Page 45   *Quel est le plus long souterrain?*

Le plus long souterrain est/C'est le souterrain de Marion.

Page 47   What if?

*Je dépenserais tout!
Je ferais réparer le toit.
Tu aurais une nouvelle bicyclette.
Nous irions tous voir ma tante au Canada.*

Page 48   Marion's letter

Monday 2 September

Dear Luc and Céline,
Here's the article from The Tourville Echo that tells our story. It's brilliant! What are you going to do with your share of the reward? I'm going to buy a radio-cassette with mine.

If your Mum agrees, I'll come to your place during the Christmas holidays, so see you soon, I hope!
Love, Marion

The newspaper article

The Camembert family treasure.

Marion Camembert with her friends Luc and Céline Meunier and her dog, Toudou.

Félix Filou, the rare bird thief who wanted to steal the Camembert family treasure.

For Marion Camembert and her friends Luc and Céline, August has been an exciting month. They found some treasure and helped the police to catch a crook, Félix Filou.
    A few months ago, Filou was on one of the Wazorare islands. He was looking for some very rare parrots there that he wanted to steal. He came across a letter from Marion's great-grandfather, Clément. It was an old letter addressed to Marion's grandfather, Joseph, and left on the island in an old chest after Clément's death. The letter was the first clue in a treasure hunt. It brought Filou to Tourville where, stupidly, he lost it. Luc and Céline, who were coming to spend a few days with their friend Marion, found it. The three teenagers managed to find the treasure (gold), hidden in the old Pirates' Fort, before the crook, and they helped the police to catch him.
    The three heroes also received a reward of 15 000 francs from the police. Our congratulations to them!

Numbers and other useful words

Here you will find some useful lists of words and expressions. Remember that telling the time is explained on page 24 and directions are on page 15.

Essential expressions

bonjour	hello, good morning
bonsoir	good evening, good night
bonne nuit	good night
au revoir	goodbye
salut	hi, bye
à bientôt	see you soon
à tout à l'heure	see you later
oui	yes
non	no
peut-être	maybe
s'il te plaît, s'il vous plaît	please
merci (beaucoup)	thank you (very much)
pardon	excuse me
Je suis désolé(e).	I'm sorry.
Je vous en prie.	You're welcome.
Je ne comprends pas.	I don't understand.
Je ne sais pas.	I don't know.
Que veut dire ce mot?	What does this word mean?
Comment dit-on ça en français?	What's the French for this?

Numbers

0	*zéro*	18	*dix-huit*
1	*un*	19	*dix-neuf*
2	*deux*	20	*vingt*
3	*trois*	21	*vingt et un*
4	*quatre*	22	*vingt-deux*
5	*cinq*	23	*vingt-trois*
6	*six*	30	*trente*
7	*sept*	31	*trente et un*
8	*huit*	40	*quarante*
9	*neuf*	50	*cinquante*
10	*dix*	60	*soixante*
11	*onze*	70	*soixante-dix*
12	*douze*	71	*soixante et onze*
13	*treize*	72	*soixante-douze*
14	*quatorze*	80	*quatre-vingts*
15	*quinze*	81	*quatre-vingt-un*
16	*seize*	90	*quatre-vingt-dix*
17	*dix-sept*	91	*quatre-vingt-onze*

100	*cent*
101	*cent un*
150	*cent cinquante*
200	*deux cents*
201	*deux cent un*
300	*trois cents*

1 000	*mille*
1 100	*onze cents, mille cent*
1 200	*douze cents, mille deux cents*
2 000	*deux mille*
2 100	*deux mille cent*
10 000	*dix mille*
100 000	*cent mille*
1 000 000	*un million*

"First", "second", "third", etc.

The French for "first" is *premier* (*première* in the feminine). For all other numbers, you simply add *-ième* to the number, although with numbers that end in "e", you drop the "e" before adding *-ième* and the "f" of *neuf* changes to "v":

(le) premier, (la) première	(the) first
(le/la) deuxième	(the) second
(le/la) troisième	(the) third
(le/la) neuvième	(the) ninth

Months, seasons and days

janvier	January
février	February
mars	March
avril	April
mai	May
juin	June
juillet	July
août	August
septembre	September
octobre	October
novembre	November
décembre	December
le printemps	spring
l'été [m]	summer
l'automne [m]	autumn
l'hiver [m]	winter
lundi [m]	Monday
mardi [m]	Tuesday
mercredi [m]	Wednesday
jeudi [m]	Thursday
vendredi [m]	Friday
samedi [m]	Saturday
dimanche [m]	Sunday
le mois	month
la saison	season
l'an [m], *l'année* [f]	year
le jour	day
la semaine	week
le week-end	week-end
hier	yesterday
aujourd'hui	today

demain	tomorrow
avant-hier	the day before yesterday
après-demain	the day after tomorrow
cette semaine	this week
la semaine dernière/prochaine	last/next week

Dates

l'agenda [m]	diary
le calendrier	calendar
Quelle est la date?	What's the date?
le lundi	on Monday
en août, au mois d'août	in August
le premier avril	1st April
le deux janvier	2nd January
mardi 7 septembre	Tuesday 7th September
1992	*mille neuf cent quatre-vingt-douze*
1993	*mille neuf cent quatre-vingt-treize*
1999	*mille neuf cent quatre-vingt-dix-neuf*
2000	*l'an deux mille*

Weather

le temps	weather
le climat	climate
la météo	weather forecast
la température	temperature
Quelle est la température?	What's the temperature?
Quel temps fait-il?	What's the weather like?
Il fait beau.	It's fine.
Il fait mauvais.	The weather's bad, It's bad weather.
Il pleut.	It's raining.
Il fait chaud.	It's hot.
Il fait du soleil.	It's sunny.
Le soleil brille.	The sun's shining.
Il fait froid.	It's cold.
Il neige.	It's snowing.
Il y a du verglas.	It's icy.
Il y a du brouillard.	It's foggy.
le ciel	sky
le soleil	sun
la pluie	rain
le nuage	cloud
la foudre	lightning
le tonnerre	thunder
le gel	frost
la neige	snow
la grêle	hail

French-English word list

This list contains all the French words from the illustrated section of this book, along with their pronunciations and English translations.

[m], **[f]**, **[pl]** and the asterisk (*) are used as throughout the book (see Key, page 3).

Nouns
Those with irregular plurals have their plural ending in curved brackets. Add the letter(s) in brackets to the noun to get the plural form. If the plural form is very different, it is given in full in brackets.

Adjectives
The feminine form is shown in brackets. Add the letter(s) in brackets to the adjective to get the feminine form. If the feminine form is very different, it is given in full in brackets.

Pronunciation
The centre column shows you how to pronounce each word. The way to say the words properly is to imitate French speakers and apply the rules given on pages 4-5. However, by reading the "words" in this column as if they were English, you will get a good idea of how to say things, or you will remember the sound of words you have heard before.

Note that, in this column, the French **u** is shown as "ew". Remember, it is a sharp "u" sound (see page 4). **E**, **eu** and **œu** are shown by "e(r)". These sounds are a bit like the "u" sound in "fur". The nasal sounds are shown by a vowel + "(n)".

A

à	*a*	in, at, to
à bientôt	*a bee-i(n)-to*	see you soon
à cause de	*a koz de(r)*	because of
à côté de	*a kotai de(r)*	next to
à droite	*a dr-wat*	(to/on the) right
à gauche	*a gosh*	(to/on the) left
à l'intérieur	*al-i(n)tai-ree-e(r)r*	inside
à la maison	*a la mai-zo(n)*	(at) home
à l'ombre	*a lo(n)br*	in the shade
à quelle heure?	*a kel e(r)r*	what time?
à qui?	*a kee*	whose?, to who(m)?
à tout à l'heure	*a too-ta-le(r)r*	see you later
à travers	*a tra-vair*	through
abandonner	*aba(n)-donai*	to abandon, to leave
*aboyer**	*abwa-yai*	to bark
adieu	*a-dee-ye(r)*	farewell
l'adolescent [m]	*la-do-lai-ssa(n)*	teenager
adorer	*ado-rai*	to adore, to love
l'adresse [f]	*la-dress*	address
adresser	*adress-ai*	to address
l'aéroport [m]	*la-ai-ro-por*	airport
les affaires [f]	*laiz-af-air*	things
l'agenda [m]	*la-ju(n)da*	diary
aider	*ai-dai*	to help
aimer	*ai-mai*	to like, to love
*aller**	*alai*	to go
allô	*a-lo*	hello (used on phone)
alors	*a-lor*	then, so, well
l'ami [m], *l'amie* [f]	*la-mee, la-mee*	friend
Amitiés	*amee-tee-ai*	Love
l'an [m], *l'année* [f]	*la(n), la-nai*	year
l'anneau(x) [m]	*la-no*	ring
...ans	*a(n)*	...years old
l'appareil-photo [m]	*la-pa-rai-y-foto*	camera
appartenir à*	*apar-te(r)-neer a*	to belong to
apporter	*apor-tai*	to bring
*apprendre**	*apra(n)-dr*	to learn
après	*aprai*	after
après-demain	*aprai-de(r)-mi(n)*	the day after tomorrow
l'arbre [m]	*lar-br*	tree
l'argent [m]	*lar-ja(n)*	money
arrêter	*arai-tai*	to stop, to arrest
l'arrière-grand-père [m]	*laree-air gra(n)-pair*	great-grandfather
arriver	*aree-vai*	to arrive, to come, to get to
l'article [m]	*lar-teekl*	article
l'aspirine [f]	*lass-pee-reen*	aspirin
assez	*assai*	quite
assez de/d'	*assai de(r)/d*	enough
l'atelier [m]	*late(r)-lee-ai*	studio
*atteindre**	*ati(n)dr*	to reach, to get to
*attendre**	*ata(n)dr*	to wait
attention	*ata(n)-see-o(n)*	watch out, careful
attraper	*atra-pai*	to catch
au bord de/d'	*obor de(r)/d*	by (the side of)
au bout de/d'	*oboo de(r)/d*	at/to the end
aujourd'hui	*ojoor-dwee*	today
aussi	*ossee*	too, also, as well, (just) as
aussi...que/qu'	*ossee ke(r)/k*	(just) as...as
autre	*otr*	other, another
avant	*ava(n)*	before
avant-hier	*ava(n)-tee-air*	the day before yesterday
avec	*avaik*	with
*avoir**	*av-wa-r*	to have
avoir besoin de/d'*	*av-wa-r be(r)-z-wi(n) de(r)/d*	to need
avoir l'air*	*av-wa-r lair*	to look, to seem, to appear

B

(gros) baisers [m]	*(gro) bai-zai*	(lots of) kisses
le banc	*le(r) ba(n)*	bench
le barreau(x)	*le(r) ba-ro*	bar (on window)
la barrière	*la bar-ee-air*	gate
les baskets [f]	*lai bass-ket*	trainers
la bataille	*la bata-ee-y*	battle
le bateau(x)	*le(r) bato*	ship, boat
le bâtiment	*le(r) batee-ma(n)*	building
bâtir	*ba-teer*	to build
beau/bel (belle)	*bo/bel (bel)*	beautiful, good-looking, fine
beaucoup de/d'	*bo-koo de(r)/d*	many, a lot of
bête	*bai-t*	stupid, daft
bêtement	*bai-te(r)-ma(n)*	stupidly
la bicyclette	*la beessee-klait*	bicycle
bien	*bee-i(n)*	well, very, most, really, so
bien sûr	*bee-i(n) sewr*	of course
bientôt	*bee-i(n)-to*	soon
le bijou(x)	*le(r) bee-joo*	piece of jewellery
la bise	*la beez*	kiss
bizarre	*bee-zar*	weird, strange, odd
la blague	*la blag*	joke
blanc(he)	*bla(n) (blansh)*	white
bleu(e)	*ble(r)*	blue
le bois	*le(r) bwa*	wood
bon(ne)	*bo(n) (bon)*	good, right, nice
le bonbon	*le(r) bo(n)-bo(n)*	sweet, candy
bonjour	*bo(n)-joor*	hello
bonnes vacances!	*bon va-ka(n)ss*	(have a) good holiday/vacation!
bonsoir	*bo(n) swar*	good evening, good-night
le botaniste	*le(r) bota-neest*	botanist
les bottes [f]	*lai bot*	boots
bouger	*boo-jai*	to move
la bougie	*la boo-jee*	candle
la boulangerie	*la boo-la(n)-je(r)-ree*	baker's
le bout	*le(r) boo*	bit, piece
briller	*bree-yai*	to shine

C

ça	*sa*	this, that
ça ne fait rien	*sa ne(r) fai-ree-i(n)*	it doesn't matter
ça suffit	*sa sew-fee*	that's enough
ça va	*sa va*	(it's) all right
cacher	*ka-shai*	to hide

se cacher	se(r) ka-shai	to hide (yourself)
le cachet	le(r) ka-shai	pill, tablet
le cachet (d'aspirine)	le(r) ka-shai (dass-pee-reen)	aspirin
le cachot	le(r) kasho	dungeon
le café	le(r) kafai	café, coffee
se calmer	se(r) kal-mai	to calm down
le camembert	le(r) kama(n)-bair	camembert (a French cheese)
le camping	le(r) ka(n)peeng	campsite
le Canada	le(r) Kanada	Canada
le carrefour	le(r) kar-foor	junction
la carte	la kart	map
la carte (à jouer)	la kart (a-joo-ai)	(playing) card
la carte postale	la kart poss-tal	postcard
le carton	le(r) karto(n)	(cardboard) box
la casquette	la kass-ket	cap
cassé(e)	kassai	broken
casser	kassai	to break (something)
se casser	se(r) kassai	to break
ce, c'	se(r), s	this, that
ce/cet, cette (ces)	se(r)/sait, sait (sai)	this, that (those)
ce matin	se(r) mati(n)	this morning
ce sont	se(r) so(n)	they are, these/those are
cela	sela	this, that
celle-ci, celle-là [f]	sel-see, sel-la	this one, that one
celles-ci, celles-là [f pl]	sel-see, sel-la	these ones, those ones
celui-ci, celui-là [m]	se(r)l-wee-see, se(r)l-wee-la	this one, that one
cent	sa(n)	a hundred
certainement	ser-tain-ma(n)	certainly, definitely
ces	sai	these, those
c'est	sai	it is, this/that is
ceux-ci, ceux-là [m pl]	se(r)-see, se(r)-la	these ones, those ones
la chambre	la sha(n)br	(bed)room
le champ	le(r) sha(n)	field
changer	sha(n)jai	to change
la chanson	la sha(n)sso(n)	song
chanter	sha(n)tai	to sing
le chapeau(x)	le(r) shapo	hat
le chapeau(x) haut de forme	le(r) shapo-o-de(r) for-m	top hat
chaque	shak	each
la chasse au trésor	la shass-o-traiz-or	treasure hunt
chasser	shassai	to chase (away), to expel
le chat	le(r) sha	cat
le château(x)	le(r) shato	castle
chaud(e)	sho	warm
la chaussette	la shosset	sock
la chaussure	la shossewr	shoe
chauve	shov	bald
le chemin	le(r) she(r)-mi(n)	path, lane, way
la chemise	la she(r)-meez	shirt
cher (chère)	shair (shair)	dear, expensive
chercher	shair-shai	to look for
chéri [m], chérie [f]	shai-ree, shai-ree	darling, dear
la chèvre	la shaivr	goat
chez	shai	at the house of, at ...'s
chez moi/toi, etc.	shai mwa/twa	at my/your, etc. place
le chien	le(r) shee-i(n)	dog
choisir	shwa-zeer	to choose
chouette	shoo-ait	great
le ciel	le(r) see-ail	sky
le cinéma	le(r) see-nai-ma	cinema
la clé	la klai	key
la clôture	la klo-tewr	fence
le coca	le(r) koka	cola
le coffre	le(r) kofr	chest (container)
le coffre-fort	le(r) kofr-for	safe
le collant	le(r) kol-a(n)	tights
la collection	la kolek-see-o(n)	collection
la colline	la ko-leen	hill
combien (de + noun)	ko(n)bee-i(n) (de(r))	how much, how many
comme	kom	as (a/the), like
comment	kom-a(n)	how
comprendre*	ko(n)-pra(n)dr	to understand
connaître*	konaitr	to know
content(e)	ko(n)-ta(n)	pleased, happy
continuer	ko(n)-teen-ew-ai	to carry on, to continue

contre	ko(n)tr	against
le copain, la copine	le(r) kopi(n), la kopeen	mate, good friend
la corde	la kord	rope
le costume	le(r) koss-tewm	suit
la côte	la kot	coast
se coucher	se(r) koo-shai	to go to bed
couper	koo-pai	to cut
le couple	le(r) koopl	couple, pair
court(e)	koor	short
coûter	kootai	to cost
le crabe	le(r) krab	crab
le crayon (de couleur)	le(r) krai-yo(n) (de(r) koo-le(r)r)	crayon
le croissant	le(r) kr-wassa(n)	croissant

D

d'abord	dabor	first of all
dangereux (dangereuse)	da(n)-je(r)-re(r) (da(n)-je(r)-re(r)z)	dangerous
dans	da(n)	in, into
de/d'	de(r)/d	of, from
de temps en temps	de(r) ta(n)-za(n)-ta(n)	sometimes
le dé	le(r) dai	die (pl dice)
déchiffrer	daishee-frai	to decipher, to work out
déchirer	daishee-rai	to tear (up)
dedans	de(r)-da(n)	inside
dehors	de(r)-or	outside
déjà	dai-ja	already
le déjeuner	le(r) dai-je(r)-nai	lunch
demain	de(r)-mi(n)	tomorrow
demain matin	de(r)-mi(n) mati(n)	tomorrow morning
demander	de(r)-ma(n)-dai	to ask
se dépêcher	se(r) daipaishai	to hurry (up)
dépenser	daipa(n)-sai	to spend
déranger	daira(n)-jai	to disturb
dernier (dernière)	dair-nee-ai (dair-nee-air)	last
derrière	dair-ee-air	behind
dès que/qu'	dai ke(r)/k	as soon as
descendre*	daissa(n)dr	to go down(stairs)
désert(e)	daizair	deserted, desert
le dessin	le(r) daissi(n)	drawing
dessiner	daisseenai	to draw
dessus	de(r)ssew	on top of (it), on (it)
le détail	le(r) daita-y	detail
détruire*	daitr-weer	to destroy
deux	de(r)	two
deuxième	de(r)zee-aim	second
devant	de(r)va(n)	in front of
devenir*	de(r)-ve(r)-neer	to become
devoir*	de(r)v-war	to have to, must
d'habitude	dabeetewd	usually, normally
difficile	deefeesseel	difficult
dîner	dee-nai	to have supper
la direction	la deerek-see-o(n)	direction
disparaître*	deess-paraitr	to disappear
la disparition	la deess-pa-ree-see-o(n)	disappearance
donc	do(n)k	so, therefore
dormir*	dormeer	to sleep, to be asleep
doucement	dooss-ma(n)	slowly
droite	drwat	right
du, de la, de l', des	dew, de(r) la, de(r) l, dai	some, any, of the

E

l'écho [m]	lai-ko	echo
l'école [f]	laikol	school
l'église [f]	laigleez	church
elle	ail	she, it
elles	ail	they
éloigné(e)	ail-wan-yai	remote, far away
emballer	a(n)balai	to wrap (up)
emporter	a(n)portai	to take (away)

emprunter	*a(n)pru(n)-tai*	to borrow
en	*a(n)*	in (before a language, colour, season or month), some, any
en dessous	*a(n) dessoo*	underneath
en face de	*a(n) fass de(r)*	opposite
en ruine	*a(n) rew-een*	ruined, in ruins
encore	*a(n)-kor*	even, again, more
l'endroit [m]	*la(n)-dr-wa*	place
l'enfant [m]	*la(n)-fa(n)*	child
enfin	*a(n)-fi(n)*	at last, anyhow
entendre*	*a(n)-ta(n)dr*	to hear
entre	*a(n)tr*	between
l'entrée [f]	*la(n)-trai*	entrance
entrer	*a(n)trai*	to go in, to enter, to come in
envoyer*	*a(n)v-wa-yai*	to send
l'escroc [m]	*less-kro*	crook
espérer	*ess-pairai*	to hope
et	*ai*	and
et puis	*ai pwee*	and then, and also, and anyhow
les États-Unis [m]	*laiz-aitaz-ewnee*	United States
l'été [m]	*laitai*	summer
être*	*aitr*	to be
être* **d'accord**	*aitr dakor*	to agree
étudier	*aitew-dee-ai*	to study
exactement	*exakte(r)ma(n)*	exactly
exagérer	*exajairai*	to exaggerate, to go too far, to push your luck
examiner	*exameenai*	to examine
l'excursion [f]	*lex-kewr-see-o(n)*	outing, trip
expliquer	*explee-kai*	to explain
explorer	*explorai*	to explore

F

facile	*fasseel*	easy, simple
faire*	*fair*	to do
faire* **attention**	*fair ata(n)-see-o(n)*	to watch out, be careful
faire* **des courses**	*fair dai koorss*	to do some shopping
faire* **nuit**	*fair new-ee*	to be night-time/dark
faire* **réparer**	*fair raiparai*	to have mended
la famille	*la famee-y*	family
fatigué(e)	*fateegai*	tired
faux (fausse)	*fo (foss)*	false
faxer	*faxai*	to fax, to send a fax
féliciter	*failee-see-tai*	to congratulate
la femme	*la fam*	woman
la fenêtre	*la fe(r)-naitr*	window
le fer	*le(r) fair*	iron
la ferme	*la fairm*	farm
fermé(e)	*fairmai*	closed
fermé(e) à clé	*fairmai a klai*	locked
fermer	*fair-mai*	to close, to shut
la feuille	*la fe(r)-y*	leaf, sheet (of paper)
les feux [m]	*lai fe(r)*	traffic lights
le filet	*le(r) fee-lai*	net
la fille	*la fee-y*	girl, daughter
le fils	*le(r) feess*	son
finir	*fee-neer*	to finish
la fontaine	*la fo(n)-tain*	fountain
la forêt	*la fo-rai*	forest
fort	*for*	loud(ly)
fort(e)	*for*	strong
le fort	*le(r) for*	fort
la fortune	*la for-tewn*	fortune
la fraise	*la fraiz*	strawberry
le franc	*le(r) fra(n)*	franc
la France	*la fra(n)ss*	France
le frère	*le(r) frair*	brother
les frites [f]	*lai freet*	chips, French fries
le fromage	*le(r) fro-maj*	cheese

G

gagner	*gan-yai*	to win, to earn
le garçon	*le(r) gar-so(n)*	boy
garder	*gar-dai*	to keep
la gare	*la gar*	station
le gâteau(x)	*le(r) gato*	cake
gauche	*gosh*	left
le gendarme	*le(r) ja(n)-darm*	policeman
la gendarmerie	*la ja(n)dar-me(r)-ree*	police station
gêner	*jainai*	to bother, to be/get in the way
génial(e)	*jainee-al*	brilliant
gentil(le)	*ja(n)-tee (ja(n)tee-y)*	kind, nice
la glace	*la glass*	ice cream
glacé(e)	*glassai*	ice-cold
le gosse	*le(r) goss*	kid
goûter	*gootai*	to taste, to have a taste
le gouverneur	*le(r) goovair-ne(r)-r*	governor
la grand-mère	*la gra(n)-mair*	grand-mother
le grand-père	*le(r) gra(n)-pair*	grand-father
grand(e)	*gra(n)*	big, large, tall
la (grande) route	*la (gra(n)d) root*	(main) road
le grenier	*le(r) gre(r)-nee-ai*	attic
la grille	*la gree-y*	gate
gris(e)	*gree*	grey
gros(se)	*gro (gross)*	big, large, fat
la grotte	*la grot*	cave

H

s'habiller	*sabee-yai*	to dress, to get dressed
l'habitant [m]	*labee-ta(n)t*	inhabitant
habiter	*abeetai*	to live
le haut-de-forme	*le(r) o-de(r)-form*	top hat
le héros	*le(r) airo*	hero
l'heure [f]	*le(r)r*	hour
... heures	*le(r)r*	... o'clock
heureusement	*he(r)-re(r)z-ma(n)*	luckily, happily, fortunately
hier	*ee-air*	yesterday
hier soir	*ee-air swar*	yesterday evening, last night
l'histoire [f]	*leess-twar*	story, history
l'homme [m]	*lom*	man
hors de	*or-de(r)*	out of
l'hôtel [m]	*lo-tel*	hotel
huit	*weet*	eight

I

ici	*eessee*	here
l'idée [f]	*lee-dai*	idea
il	*eel*	he/it
il est interdit de/d'	*eel ait-i(n)tair-dee de(r)/d*	it is forbidden to
il faut	*eel fo*	you/we/one must, it is necessary to
il pleut	*eel ple(r)*	it is raining/it rains
il s'appelle	*eel-sapel*	his/its name is (he/it is called)
il y a	*eel-ee-a*	there is/are, ago
l'île [f]	*leel*	island
ils	*eel*	they
impossible	*i(n)posseebl*	impossible
l'indice [m]	*li(n)-deess*	clue
s'inquiéter	*si(n)-kee-aitai*	to worry
l'instituteur [m]	*li(n)stee-tew-te(r)r*	(junior school) teacher
intéressant(e)	*i(n)tai-raissa(n)*	interesting

J

jamais (ne...jamais)	*jamai (ne(r) jamai)*	never (not ever)
le Japon	*le(r) japo(n)*	Japan

le jardin	le(r) jardi(n)	garden
le jardin public	le(r) jardi(n) pew-bleek	park
jaune	jon	yellow
je, j'	je(r), j	I
je m'appelle	je(r) mapel	my name is (I am called)
le jean	le(r) djeen	jeans
joli(e)	jolee	pretty
le jour	le(r) joor	day
le journal (journaux)	le(r) joornal (joorno)	newspaper
la journée	la joor-nai	day
les jumelles [f]	lai jew-mel	binoculars
la jupe	la jewp	skirt
le jus d'orange	le(r) jew do-ra(n)j	orange juice
jusqu'à	jewss-ka	as far as, up/down to, until

K

le kilo (de/d'...)	le(r) keelo (de(r)/d)	kilo of

L

là	la	there
là-bas	la-ba	over there
le lac	le(r) lak	lake
laisser	laissai	to leave (behind)
la lampe (de poche)	la la(n)p (de(r) posh)	torch, flashlight
lancer	la(n)ssai	to throw
se laver	se(r) lavai	to have a wash, to get washed
le, la, l', les	le(r), la, l, lai	the
le légume	le(r) laigewm	vegetable
lent(e)	la(n)	slow
lentement	la(n)t-ma(n)	slowly
la lettre	la letr	letter
se lever	se(r) le(r)-vai	to get up
la lime	la leem	nail file
la limonade	la leemonad	lemonade
lire*	leer	to read
le livre	le(r) leevr	book
le locataire	le(r) lokatair	lodger
loin de	lwi(n) de(r)	far from
long(ue)	lo(n) (lo(n)g)	long
lors de	lor de(r)	at the time of
louer	loo-ai	to hire, to rent
la loupe	la loop	magnifying glass
la lumière	la lew-mee-air	light
lundi	lu(n)-dee	Monday
les lunettes [f]	lai lewnet	glasses

M

le maçon	le(r) masso(n)	builder
Madame	ma-dam	Mrs
Mademoiselle	ma-de(r)m-wa-zel	Miss
le magasin	le(r) magazi(n)	shop
le magicien	le(r) majeessee-i(n)	magician
maintenant	mi(n)te(r)-na(n)	now
mais	mai	but
la maison	la maizo(n)	house
mal	mal	badly
malade	malad	ill, unwell
malheureusement	male(r)-re(r)z-ma(n)	unfortunately, sadly
Maman	mama(n)	Mum, Mummy
la mandarine	la ma(n)dareen	mandarin
manger	ma(n)jai	to eat
manquer	ma(n)kai	to be missing
la marche	la marsh	step
le marché	le(r) marshai	market
marcher	marshai	to walk
mardi	mardee	Tuesday
marron	maro(n)	brown
mauvais(e)	movai	wrong, bad

le mécanicien	le(r) maikaneess-ee-i(n)	mechanic
meilleur(e)	mai-ye(r)r	better
le/la/les meilleur(e)(s)	le(r)/la/lai mai-ye(r)r	the best
le/la/les même(s)	le(r)/la/lai maim	the (very) same
mener	me(r)nai	to lead, to bring
mentir*	ma(n)teer	to lie (tell lies)
la mer	la mair	the sea
merci	mair-see	thank you
la mère	la mair	mother
mettre*	metr	to put
mettre* de l'ordre	metr de(r) lordr	to tidy up
midi	meedee	midday
mieux, le mieux	mee-ye(r), le(r) mee-ye(r)	better, the best
minuit	meen-wee	midnight
moche	mosh	horrible, ugly
moi	mwa	me, as for me
moins, le moins	mwi(n), le(r) mwi(n)	fewer/less, fewest/least
le mois	le(r) mwa	month
Monsieur	me(r)ssee-ye(r)	Mr
la montagne	la mo(n)tan-y	mountain
monter	mo(n)tai	to go up(stairs)
montrer	mo(n)trai	to show
le monument	le(r) monew-ma(n)	monument
le morceau(x)	le(r) mor-so	piece
mort(e)	mor	dead
la mort	la mor	death
le mot	le(r) mo	word, note
mouillé(e)	moo-yai	wet
mourir*	mooreer	to die
le mur	le(r) mewr	wall

N

naître	naitr	to be born
ne...pas	ne(r) pa	not
ne...pas de/d'	ne(r) pa de(r)/d	not a, not any, no
ne...pas encore	ne(r) paza(n)kor	not yet
ne...personne	ne(r) pair-son	not...anybody, nobody
ne...plus	ne(r) plew	not any more, no longer
ne...rien	ne(r) ree-i(n)	not...anything, nothing
Noël	no-ail	Christmas
noir(e)	nwar	black
non	no(n)	no
nous	noo	we
nouveau/nouvel/ nouvelle	noovo/noovail/ noovail	new
la nuit	la nwee	night
nulle part	newl par	nowhere
le numéro	le(r) newmairo	number

O

l'objet [m]	lobjai	object, thing
l'œuf [m] (les œufs)	le(r)f (laiz-e(r))	egg
offrir*	ofreer	to treat (someone to), to give, to offer
oh là!	o-la	oh no!, oh dear!
l'oiseau(x) [m]	lwazo	bird
l'ombre [f]	lo(n)br	shade, shadow
on	o(n)	we, one, you
l'or [m]	lor	gold
l'orange [f]	loranj	orange
l'oreille [f]	lorai-y	ear
où	oo	where
oublier	ooblee-ai	to forget
oui	wee	yes
l'outil [m]	loo-tee	tool
ouvrir*	oovreer	to open

P

le pain	le(r) pi(n)	bread
la paire	la pair	pair

French	Pronunciation	English
le panier	le(r) pa-nee-ai	basket
le panneau(x)	le(r) pa-no	panel
le pantalon	le(r) pa(n)talo(n)	trousers
Papa	papa	Dad, Daddy
le papier	le(r) papee-ai	paper
par	par	by, through (a window)
par ici	paree-see	this way, over/around here
par là	par la	that way, over/around there
parce que	parss-ke(r)	because
pardon	pardo(n)	sorry, excuse me
pareil(le)	parai-y (parai-y)	(the) same
les parents [m]	lai para(n)	parents
parfait(e)	parfai	perfect
parfois	parfwa	sometimes
le parfum	le(r) parfu(n)	flavour
parler	par-lai	to talk, to speak
la part	la par	part, share
partir*	parteer	to go (away), to leave
partout	partoo	everywhere
pas	pa	not
le passage clouté	le(r) passaj clootai	pedestrian crossing
passer	passai	to pass, to spend (time), to hand
passionnant(e)	passee-ona(n)	exciting
payer*	pa-yai	to pay
le pays	le(r) pai-yee	country
le paysage	le(r) pai-yee-zaj	landscape
pendant	pa(n)da(n)	during
penser	pa(n)-sai	to think
perdre*	pairdr	to lose
le père	le(r) pair	father
le perroquet	le(r) pairokai	parrot
personne	pair-son	nobody
petit(e)	pe(r)-tee	small, little, short
peu	pe(r)	few, little
peut-être	pe(r)-taitr	maybe, perhaps
la pharmacie	la farmassee	chemist's, pharmacy
la photo	la foto	photo
la photocopieuse	la fotokopee-e(r)z	photocopier
la pièce	la pee-aiss	room, part
le piège	le(r) pee-aij	trap
la pierre	la pee-air	rock, stone
le pirate	le(r) pee-rat	pirate
pire, le/la/les pire(s)	peer, le(r)/la/lai peer	worse, the worst
la piscine	la peesseen	swimming pool
la piste	la peesst	trail, piste
la place	la plass	square
la plage	la plaj	beach
la plante	la pla(n)t	plant
plein(e)	pli(n) (plain)	full
plein de/d'	pli(n) de(r)/d	lots of
la pluie	la plwee	rain
plus	plew (or plewss)	more
le/la/les plus	le(r)/la/lai plew	the most
la poche	la posh	pocket
le pôle	le(r) pol	pole
la police	la poleess	police
la pomme	la pom	apple
le pont	le(r) po(n)	bridge
le port	le(r) por	port
la porte	la port	door
porter	portai	to carry, to wear
le portrait	le(r) portrai	portrait
poser	pozai	to put down
la poste	la posst	post office
pour	poor	for, in order to, so as to, to
pourquoi	poorkwa	why
pouvoir*	poov-war	to be able to, can, may
préféré(e)	praifairai	favourite
(le) premier, (la) première	(le(r)) pre(r)-mee-yai, (la) pre(r)mee-yair	(the) first
prendre*	pra(n)dr	to take
(tout) près de	(too) prai de(r)	(right) near
presque	pressk	almost, nearly
prêt(e)	prai	ready
prêter	praitai	to lend
probablement	probabl-ma(n)	probably
prochain(e)	proshi(n)	next
le propriétaire	le(r) propree-ai-tair	owner, landlord
le pull	le(r) pewl	jumper

Q

French	Pronunciation	English
le quai	le(r) kai	quay
quand	ka(n)	when
quatrième	katree-aim	fourth
que (qu')	ke(r) (k)	who(m), which, what, than
quel(le)	kel	which, what
quelle heure est-il?	kel e(r)r-ait-eel	what time is it?, what's the time?
quelque chose	kelke(r) shoz	something
quelque part	kelke(r) par	somewhere
quelques	kelke(r)	a few
qu'est-ce que (c'est)?	kess-ke(r) (ssai)	what (is it/this/that)?
la question	la kess-tee-o(n)	question
qui	kee	who, which

R

French	Pronunciation	English
raconter	ra-ko(n)-tai	to tell
la radiocassette	la radee-o-kassait	radio cassette
la rame	la ram	oar
ramer	ra-mai	to row
ranger	ra(n)-jai	to put away
rapporter	raportai	to bring/take back
rare	rar	rare
se raser	se(r) razai	to shave
recevoir*	re(r)ss-e(r)-vwar	to receive, to get
recherché(e)	re(r)-shair-shai	sought after, wanted
recommander	re(r)-koma(n)-dai	to recommend
la récompense	la rai-ko(n)-pa(n)ss	reward
reconnaître*	re(r)-konaitr	to recognize
réfléchir	rai-flai-sheer	to think
regarder	re(r)-gar-dai	to look at
remercier	re(r)-mair-see-ai	to thank
rentrer	ra(n)-trai	to come/go (back/home)
réparer	rai-pa-rai	to repair, to mend
la réponse	la rai-ponss	answer
le restaurant	le(r) raiss-to-ra(n)	restaurant
rester	raiss-tai	to stay, to remain
retourner	re(r)-toor-nai	to go back
retrouver	re(r)-troo-vai	to find (again), to track down
la réunion	la rai-ew-nee-yo(n)	meeting
réussir (à)	rai-ewssir (a)	to manage (to), to succeed (in)
se réveiller	se(r) rai-vai-yai	to wake up
revenir*	re(r)-ve(r)-neer	to come back, to return
riche	reesh	rich, wealthy
rien	ree-i(n)	nothing
la rivière	la ree-vee-air	river
la robe	la rob	dress
rouge	rooj	red
rouillé(e)	roo-yai	rusty
la route	la root	road
le ruban	le(r) rew-ba(n)	ribbon
la rue	la rew	street
la ruine	la rween	ruin

S

French	Pronunciation	English
le sac	le(r) sak	bag
le sac à dos	le(r) sa-ka-do	backpack, rucksack
sacré(e)	sa-krai	sacred
sage	saj	well behaved, good
la saison des tempêtes	la sai-zo(n) dai ta(n)-pait	stormy season
le salaire	le(r) sal-air	pay, salary, fee
sale	sal	dirty, horrible
salir	sa-leer	to dirty
salut	sa-lew	hi, hello, bye

(bien) s'amuser	(bee-in(n)) sa-mew-zai	to have (lots of) fun
savoir*	sav-war	to know
le secret	le(r) se(r)-krai	secret
sentir*	sa(n)-teer	to feel, to smell
se sentir* bien/mal	se(r) sa(n)-teer bee-i(n)/mal	to feel well/not well
la serrure	la sair-ewr	lock
la serviette	la sair-vee-ait	briefcase, towel
servir*	sair-veer	to serve
seul(e)	se(r)l	alone
seulement	se(r)l-ma(n)	only
le short	le(r) short	shorts
si	see	so, if
le signe	le(r) seen-y	sign
s'il te/vous plaît	seel te(r)/voo plai	please
la sœur	la se(r)r	sister
le soir	le(r) swar	evening
le soleil	le(r) so-lai-ee-y	sun
la sortie	la sortee	exit
sortir*	sor-teer	to go out
la soupe	la soop	soup
sous	soo	under
le souterrain	le(r) soo-tair-i(n)	underground passage, tunnel
souvent	soo-va(n)	often
le sparadrap	le(r) sparadra	plaster
le stylo	le(r) steelo	pen
suivre*	sweevr	to follow
le supermarché	le(r) sew-pair-mar-shai	supermarket
sur	sewr	on, onto
le survêtement	le(r) sewr-vait-ma(n)	tracksuit
le sweat-shirt	le(r) swait-shirt	sweatshirt
sympa(thique)	si(n)-pa(-teek)	nice

T

la table	la tabl	table
le tableau(x)	le(r) ta-blo	painting
la tâche	la tash	task
se taire*	se(r) tair	to be quiet
tant pis	ta(n) pee	too bad
la tante	la ta(n)t	aunt
tard	tar	late
le tee-shirt	le(r) tee-shirt	T-shirt
le temple	le(r) ta(n)pl	temple
tenir*	te(r)-neer	to hold
la tente	la ta(n)t	tent
se terminer	se(r) tair-mee-nai	to end, to finish
la terre	la tair	earth, soil
le thé	le(r) tai	tea
tirer	teerai	to pull
le toit	le(r) twa	roof
tomber	to(n)-bai	to fall (over)
tomber dans le piège	to(n)-bai da(n) le(r) pee-aij	to fall in the trap, to fall for it
tomber sur	to(n)-bai sewr	to find by chance, to come across
toujours	toojoor	always
la tour	la toor	tower
tourner	toornai	to turn
tourner en rond	toornai a(n) ro(n)	to go around in (a) circle(s)
tout	too	everything
tout de suite	too de(r) sweet	straight/right away, this instant
tout droit	too drwa	straight ahead
tout le monde	too le(r) mo(n)d	everyone, everybody
tout(e) seul(e)	too se(r)l	all alone

le train	le(r) tri(n)	train
tranquille	tra(n)-keel	quiet, calm
le travail (travaux)	le(r) tra-va-ee-y (travo)	work
travailler	tra-va-ee-yai	to work
la traversée	la travair-sai	crossing
traverser	travair-sai	to cross
très	trai	very
le trésor	le(r) trai-zor	treasure
troisième	trwa-zee-aim	third
trop	tro	too
trouver	troovai	to find
se trouver	se(r) troovai	to be, to be found/situated
tu	tew	you

U

un(e)	u(n) (ewn)	a, an, one

V

les vacances [f]	lai vaka(n)ss	holidays, vacations
la vache	la vash	cow
la valise	la valeez	suitcase
le veau(x)	le(r) vo	calf
vénérer	vai-nai-rai	to worship
se venger	se(r) va(n)-jai	to get your revenge
venir*	ve(r)-neer	to come
vers	vair	towards
vert(e)	vair	green
la veste	la vaisst	jacket
les vêtements [m]	lai vait-ma(n)	clothes
vide	veed	empty
vieux/vieil (vieille)	vee-e(r)/vee-ai-eey (vee-ai-eey)	old
le village	le(r) veelaj	village
la ville	la veel	town
visiter	vee-zee-tai	to visit
vite	veet	quickly, fast
la vitre	la veetr	window pane
voici	vwa-see	here's, here are
voilà	vwa-la	there's, there are
voir*	vwar	to see
le voisin	le(r) vwa-zi(n)	neighbour
la voiture	la vwa-tewr	car
le vol	le(r) vol	theft
voler	volai	to steal, to rob
le voleur	le(r) vol-e(r)r	burglar, thief
Voudriez-vous?	voo-dree-ai-voo	Would you like?
Voulez-vous?	voo-lai-voo	Do you want?
vouloir*	voo-lwar	to want
vous	voo	you
vrai(e)	vrai	true
vraiment	vrai-ma(n)	really

Y

y	ee	there

Z

zut	zewt	blast, damn

First published in 1992 by Usborne Publishing Ltd.
Usborne House, 83–85 Saffron Hill, London EC1N 8RT, England
Copyright © 1992 Usborne Publishing Ltd.

Printed in Great Britain.